HOW ONE
SAVE T

Luke Maguire Armstrong

How One Guitar Will Save the World

How One Guitar Will Save the World

Luke Maguire Armstrong

How One Guitar Will Save the World

Copyright © 2021 Luke Maguire Armstrong

Author photo by Erica Derrickson

Cover Design by Meru Campos

Set in Garamond

Pañña Press

All rights reserved.

Yet,

feel free to share parts and cite. Life's too short to worry about copyright infringement.

~All stories belong to us all~

ISBN: 9798782027889

DEDICATION

Dedicated to you dear reader. May your journey be long and bright.

And to Aaron, elder brother, teacher, friend.

First Soft Cover Edition
First Printing

How One Guitar Will Save the World

How One Guitar Will Save the World

How One Guitar Will Save the World

THANKS AND GRATITUDE

Books are our friends—a good book, a great friend. And when you're writing a book, all the characters within it are your friends, maybe some your antagonists. They live their lives through you as long as the book is coming to life by you. I remember when Liam first showed up. He was one of three characters I scrawled into my journal on a chicken bus on a dust road in Nicaragua, headed north.

Later Liam appeared in a short story written just after I settled in Antigua, Guatemala from post-graduation rambling. That story, which went on to become the first chapter of this book, was set in Eugene, Oregon. Yet like my own life, the narrative would soon make its way to its primary setting: Antigua.

I remember on a broken-down sailboat off the coast of Belize writing several key pages of this book in a sea-licked notebook. The final drafting of HOGWSTW occurred on the dash of my brother Tyler's Kia named Rio, as we put 20,000 miles and the rest of our lives into a three-month road trip that transitioned

me into life back in the US after four years working for a nonprofit in Antigua.

And then life went on. I was living in New York City sending out submissions to agents and editors. The pile of rejections came in as they do—one small publisher actually said yes, but it ended up falling through and this novel went on the shelf for the next nine years. But this year, emboldened by an enthusiastic audience, motivated be a deep plea to not forget the things I once gave my heart to—the book found its way back to my front burner and I gave it a final finessing before publishing it in the world

Dear novel—teacher and friend—I set you and all your characters into the world. May you all find a warm home in some readers' hearts.

Much gratitude is due for a work like this to survive. I'm thankful for Antigua, Guatemala—the setting of much of my adult life. Grateful for the many colorful characters and stories in those days that frequented the same taverns. Grateful to my tavern of that time, Henrik's Reilly's Pub (the real one, by the arch [a few reading will remember]).

Much gratitude is due to my cast of kind proofreaders, content editors, and copy editors. In the order I recall your reading, thank you: Emily Jacobs, Krista Steffen, Alex Ferrar, The real Stella, Chelsey Rose, to the woman who changed her name, and the ever shining Erica Derrickson—your helpful eyes helped me walk the whole way of the path that leads a book into your hands. Thanks E for the encouragement you offered this endeavor on its final lap.

Thanks to San Cristobal, Mexico and Meru Campos—and the two of you together—and the three of us together—watching you craft the cover design from that well or artistic water you carry within.

Thanks to all the artists and ramblers and troubadours who came before and will come after.

Thanks to the many over the years who listened to me read rough drafts from notebooks laden with dust and sands from the roads and coasts of this world. Thanks to this world and to tea and stories and fires and friends and guitars and singing and Karuna and longings and loving and living your dreams.

To you, I bow.

To the many wondrous places on earth of pondering and creating, I bow. To that inner impulse of pen to paper, Caribbean nights and enduring dreams, I bow. Thanks to the wonderful ways this world writes stories through us so we can better understand what we forgot we always knew.

Thanks to you dear reader, to whom I dedicate this work—you make it fully worthwhile.

—LMA

CONTENTS

Part I
Chapter One - 2
Chapter Two - 7
Chapter Three - 13
Chapter Four - 18

Part II
Chapter Five - 21
Chapter Six - 27
Chapter Seven - 35
Chapter Eight - 43
Chapter Nine - 51
Chapter Ten - 57
Chapter Eleven - 61
Chapter Twelve - 65
Chapter Thirteen - 69
Chapter Fourteen - 72
Chapter Fifteen - 76

Part III
Chapter Sixteen - 94
Chapter Seventeen - 100
Chapter Eighteen - 119
Chapter Nineteen - 121
Chapter Twenty - 129
Chapter Twenty-One - 143
Chapter Twenty-Two - 154
Chapter Twenty-Three - 161
Chapter Twenty-Four - 163
Chapter Twenty-Five - 171
Chapter Twenty-Six - 179

CHAPTER ONE

I am alone in my Zen. My scented candles are periwinkle and tranquility. I've gone all morning without answering the call of nature, listening only to the fizzling tango of ice meeting carbonation.

My energy—it is boundless. My hardcore buff-yourself-up exercise program—mere days away from beginning. My resolve—unshaken and inspiring. Potential employers will scour the world for me. My shoes are just the right size and the potential where they could tread is limitless. From this couch, what is not possible? One man. One couch. Jack Daniels. Today, I contemplate life, so that tomorrow I can live it. Tomorrow, it all begins. I am in my Zen.

Then the door shuffles open like it's a police raid and I jump, dropping my glass. Amazingly, it does not shatter. This invincible glass! I want us to all take a moment and recognize the glass, but things happen too fast. He walks in with his girlfriend, and they are both carrying cardboard boxes. He has no time for pleasantries. Not even a good morning? Who raised this guy?

In the whiney falsetto of cartoon mice, he asks, "Have you been sitting here drinking all day?"
I was in the middle of some serious Zen, some somber introspection. Jack Daniels was merely the meditation aid. Behind him Heather stands tentatively in the doorway. She's already a parody of herself, a permanent conversation starter embarking on the marital road of Sovereignty Lost.

Just as I realize I'm out of ice, he reminds me, "You remember I'm moving out today, right?"
"Oh yes." I tell him, "All last week you roamed around the apartment giving me dirty looks, and then you made your grand announcement. At first I thought you were going to deliver me one of your inspiring lectures about how I should stop being a waste of space and get a job. Then I thought, he's going to recite his moving litany about why I do not have the right to leave dirty dishes in my own sink. And just as I suspected you were going to reel off your urban legend about how regular exercise is where happiness comes from, you looked out the

window and said, "I'm moving in with Heather."

Heather is still in the doorway holding onto her boxes like they will burst into flames if she sets them down. Theatrically she clears away some shoes and candy bar packaging and flops them down, "So, it's Tuesday and you just plan to sit around drinking all day Liam?"

I crack a smile, but I don't smile inside, "Heather, I was neither up for the start of the day nor will I be up for that magical moment when the day, abreast with itself, takes the ageless descent into su-sunset." I stutter, finding several levels of hilarity hidden within the word "abreast." But I recover before Jack Daniels can get the best of me, "So the implication, Heather, that I'll be drinking all day…well, it's wrong. I'll forgive you, but it will take time."

Mark's fire feeds off Heather's fuel, "And what the hell is this music? Are those pan flutes?"

"I'm meditating."

"Drinking an entire bottle of whisky is not meditating."

"Markarony. Would you say my bottle of Jack is half full or half empty?"

"Are you serious? It's all empty! You have a shot or two left at most. Jesus—"

"IS LORD!"

"You need help."

"Mark, I don't judge your religion's rituals."

Mark drops his boxes and kicks them to the corner I've been using to store my dirty socks and snot rags—which are the same thing. "And you know what? You even promised me, you promised me, you'd finally clean this shit up before today. I can't pack if I can't walk in here."

He tries to reduce me to an eight-year-old. Soon my mom will come to put all my toys out of reach until I learn how to pick up after myself.

He backs up to shield Heather, "I'm sorry babe, you shouldn't have to see this." Then he flashes back to me, "This is so beyond ridiculous, look at this place. This is a metaphor for your life. And what the hell is brown and all over the curtains?"

I release the most potent comeback ever, "Your mom's ridiculous."

"Good one!" And Heather makes no mistake about her oxytocin-driven allegiances.

I turn to her. "Do you think this is ridiculous?"

"You know it's ridiculous, Liam. I know you had…" She swerves towards a dangerous onramp, "…but it's time to pull yourself together."

My high school Latin finally finds a real-world application, "Ridiculous, Heather, comes from the Latin root *ridiculosus*, which means, unworthy of serious consideration, in which case, I agree."

Mark takes the high road, "Don't even talk to him. You can't have an adult conversation with him when he's like this."

"Whatever then," Heather rolls her eyes until they find Mark and soften. "Baby, I gotta get back to work, good luck with…this." She glances at me like I'm digging in her dumpster and slithers out the door.

"She's a feisty one," I say to Mark, but he ignores me and begins filling his boxes. I stop watching. Every item sparks memories from the past few years. We are not who we were then and this cannot be how it ends. He was there for the funeral. He put his hand on my shoulder and did not say anything, and that was the best thing anyone did.

But this sort of saying nothing is nothing like the silence we shared then. It can't be said we are sharing this silence, just hiding on either side of it. So to make it go away, I say, "Make sure you don't pack any of my DVDs."

He looks up from the box, "Don't worry, I'm not going to steal any of your weirdo indie-films."

"They're artsy… You know that cohabitation before marriage usually leads to divorce?"

"Noted."

I transfer from the couch to the recliner and then to the chair and ask, "You want to get a beer or something before you go?"

"If you're asking me if I want to get wasted with you, the answer is no."

"That's not what I asked." I search for more to say, "I don't think we can expect our security deposit back. Look at the carpet."

"Who's fault was that?"

"Come on, the parties were joint efforts." I leave him to pack and go to my room to dig through a pile of clothes. It's here somewhere. Someone needs to clean these clothes and now Mark won't be here to remind me to do the things that aren't getting done. But he's doing worse than that. He shouldn't have a right to hammer away at our shared past, shattering with every blow good, forgotten things.

I dig. They are in here somewhere. Nope, only a box of light bulbs that sounds like a maraca when shaken. Then I find them. The Sam's Club special box of 48 assorted condoms. "Pleasure Pack" is printed prominently on the front. The family pack of condoms for families that do not want a family.

Mark's busy taking posters off his wall. I knock on the open door.

"What?"

I cradle the box behind my back and say, "I have a going-away present for you."

"Really?" he punctuates everything with frosty, staccato tones.

I bring the box to the front. Mark looks at me like I'm a disobedient child and says, "Wow, you're an asshole to the bitter end."

He doesn't understand. "No Mark, really. I want you and Heather to have these. Lord knows I don't want you two procreating."

"Thanks." He turns his back to me and un-tacks a poster of Kobe Bryant. I set the box on his nightstand and leave. In my mind, he laughs at my joke and comments how the box won't last long. He pats me on the shoulder, takes the box and we do the guy hug that starts with a handshake and ends with an embrace. He stops packing and we go to the Missile Toe bar to grab a beer. Over it we laugh about the time we got drunk and used a ladder to drink beers on our roof. We laugh at how we both decided that we would stay up there all night and in solidarity kicked the ladder away and threw our cell phone batteries to the parking lot below. And how it started raining, but we both said we didn't care. It got so cold, but we still lasted until morning, when we shouted to a waking neighbor to put the ladder back against the side of the building. And how I got sick with pneumonia, but he didn't, and how he felt guilty about that.

We shake in disbelief at the time we drove his pickup on campus after midnight and cut down a young evergreen with a steak knife for our beer-can decorated Christmas tree. But none of this happens outside of my mind. Mark loads up his last box and asks me to help him carry his dresser, desk, and bed to the back of his pickup. I assist in silence and we leave it at an impersonal, "See you later." "Take care of yourself." Our eye contact is brief and awkward and we are glad to break it and walk away into our separated lives.

CHAPTER TWO

There is a place for people like me. That place is a bar. I resolve to go downtown, where if Petula Clark is not a liar, things will be great. But downtown is far away and without a car it's easier to just walk to the neighborhood dive bar where things are consistently mediocre.

The bartender, wearing a tight black shirt, rolls his eyes at me. "Take it easy tonight, huh?" He slides me a watered-down whisky coke and walks away. It's happy hour and the young are trying to look older; the old, younger. Everyone eyes everyone, sizing them up, seeing or not seeing them in their futures, making hypothetical journeys into each other's bedrooms, using shallow appearances to undress the soul. It's palpable, the romantic uncertainty bouncing about the room— the suspense, the anticipation, the excitement, and their shadows. I twirl a straw and search my whiskey and coke for a familiar feeling of lightness that will give me enough resolve to make things happen. I have friends here. I just need to meet them. I want to feel inspired. I need to be enlightened. I take full advantage while the drinks are two for one.

In the furthest corner there is a girl who is beautiful and I could talk to her. But I have no idea how that would turn out. I'm not ugly. I have a good face, dark hair with dark eyes. Girls used to tell me they liked this. This current flabbiness I've picked up will disappear when I start my hardcore buff-yourself-up exercise program tomorrow. Tomorrow it all begins. Or next week. Tomorrow or next week at the latest. The girl in the corner is still alone. I navigate through hypothetical outcomes and wonder what hurdles would need to be crossed to dampen the guard all girls in bars have up. But she's probably waiting for someone. Before I can decide, time runs out and the price of drinks doubles. Happy hour is over.

I have been here before, in another lifetime I lived in this body. I used to come here often with friends. In between giggling, Mark and I stole the plunger from here because we didn't have our own. It was thrilling. I know it maybe doesn't sound so exciting, but you would've had to have been there to understand. I used to come here with Lisa and Tom. I remember the clouds of smoke that used to float through the bar before the city passed a smoking ban. I used to come here with Teddy and Bill. Everyone used this place as a staging ground from which the rest of their lives branched out. I used to come here with Melissa. From this bar they embarked on careers, marriages and families, grad school and law school—on empty adult lives. I used to come here with Cathy. None of them come here anymore, just me.

  Two kids a few years younger than me pull up stools to my right and order bright-blue drinks. One of them pulls out some sort of musical dildo from his vest pocket and shows it to his fedora-wearing sidekick. Hipsters, I think, we got some hipsters coming in hot.

  The one with the fedora looks at the musical dildo and asks, "Is it different than a recorder?"

  "Oh yes," the man runs his hands across it like he's trying to arouse it, "it's a traditional Irish instrument. If you have an ear for it, you'll be able to pick it out as the instrument playing the melody much of the time in Brave Heart."

  Who says things like, 'if you have an ear for it?' Hipsters, that's who.

  Fedora is unconvinced, "It looks like a recorder."

  "Brother they were playing these long before the advent of recorders." He plays a few notes on his dildo that sound just like a recorder. I turn away to order another drink and think about when advent used to be a season. According to science, The University of Oregon produces more hipsters than any other college, which is why this musical escapade is unfolding before me. It's humiliating sharing the planet with people like this. It's because of people like this that there's murder. Between the beard, the scarf that matches his vest, and tweed shoes, he looks like he was shat out of the 1920s. They fill bars around these parts, smoking their clove cigarettes, hitting bongs but not to get high, to get enlightened, drinking exotic tea blends in triangle hats while knowing numerically how much carbon they offset by riding their bikes. Many are vegan. Which is fine, but you have to understand, there are vegans, and there are fucking vegans!

  I turn to both of them, "Hey check out this joke."

They turn away from their conversation like they've just been asked to leave their homeland. "Come on get that out of your mouth," I say, "Listen. Okay, so, there is a drunk guy walking down the street and he sees this nun, he runs over to the nun, punches her in the face, and says, 'How'd you like that Batman!'"

And lo, they actually like it. Now we have camaraderie and hilarity. The recorder/dildo guy laughs like The Count from Sesame Street, "Ah, ah, ah, ah, ah." One! One joke! "Ah, ah, ah, ah, ah."

"That's pretty good," he says, "I'm Kevin." He extends his hand to meet me and I see my whole life flash before my eyes. Suddenly the task of grabbing his hands seems commensurate to picking up a sword to go fight the enemy. And I don't know what he's touched. It looks sweaty and slimy. So let me get this straight, I am supposed to take his hand and say my name and meet him and his fedora-wearing sidekick so that we can know each other, so that we can laugh like Ho Ho Ho, so that the conversation can vacillate between the serious and the absurd and the alcohol will make us believe our empty convictions with such fervor that we'll talk of politics and the state of the world and we'll talk about talking to girls and this will be a seed that could germinate into friendship and I'll think about how I misjudged them and I'll even ask him to play his stupid Irish Tin Whistler dildo thing and tomorrow I'll tell Mark that I had a crazy night—a random night!—and we'll exchange phone numbers and become Facebook friends and I've had this same strange night so many times that's it's not strange and it's just what happens when you go out to bars and tell jokes to strangers.

I shake his hand. "I'm Liam," I say, but I'm not really sure what I mean by it. I want to do the old things in new ways. As a culture we should move away from needing to know people. We could stop people on the street to ask them to go on bike rides. We could ride bikes with them without ever shaking hands and disappear back into our own lives.

Kevin's friend's name is Stuart. I did not know that people our age had that name. I tell him this, and luckily, he finds it funny and is not offended. Not yet at least. Stuart is going to grad school for classical literature and within five minutes has me petrified that we as a culture are forgetting about Sappho's poems. Does anyone even speak Latin anymore? Is it any wonder that kids are turning to drugs and having unprotected sex with zoo animals for puppy chow?"

    These hipster kids aren't monsters, I can see that. They aren't the scum of the earth. They aren't even that bad. They both have easy smiles and seem glad to be talking to me. Kevin is going to grad school for business. I had him pegged for someone who would be majoring in some obscure liberal arts field. Over the next two drinks the three of us find our rhythm. We drink and talk, talk then drink—pop culture, local politics, sports—the usual near flung topics.

    "So, what do you do?" Stuart asks me, and I have no idea. I breathe. I order pizza. I drink so much. I feel broken inside. I don't tell my mom I love her but I do. I don't know how I got here. I don't know how I'll get out of here. But instead of answering, I withdraw Kevin's dildo-whistler-thing out of his pocket. I run my fingers along it and make a soft implication about Stuart and his sexual orientation and what they will both be doing to each other with this instrument later in the evening. I say this breezily enough that anyone who is not oversensitive would be able to see that it's harmless. It's comedy and I'm serving it up for free.

    But they are soft as kids raised by a bottle of hand lotion. Kevin grabs back his stupid recorder and attempts to shove it back into his vest pocket. But he misses his pocket, he just runs it down the length of his body.
How do just a few words set people off like this? He finally gets it in his pocket and frowns his words at me—who he doesn't even know. How could I, a stranger, bring such emotion out of someone with just a few words? When Kevin sees that Stuart has turned away from both of us he says, "This is the last time I donate my time to a loser sitting all alone at the bar."

    I extend my arm until it touches his shoulder and say again, "I was kidding dude."

    He slaps my hand away and fires his final shot. "Yeah we know, we're going to talk all night about how hilarious you are."

    "So you two will be up together all night then?" I must have the face of a muppet on when I say this, but Kevin turns away for the last time, shielding Stuart from me. I stand up to go to the bathroom, but before I make it I veer to the front door and push out into the familiar night air. I follow the midnight stillness to my own apartment and slam the innocent door shut when I'm safely inside.

Shit—forgot to pay my bar tab.
My place is trashed and Mark's move gives it a look of being freshly burglarized. Only the kitchen is clean enough to stand. I sit down at my table and listen to the refrigerator breathe, waiting calmly for the day to die. Somewhere between morning and night my apartment becomes a world away from all the other worlds I know. Lately, I've been accumulating credit card debt and waiting for 3 AM. The night owls have gone to rest and the early bird still sleeps, dreaming of her worm. It's in this world that I've categorized a dozen kinds of silence. I want to stay like this forever, a silent pioneer, discovering quiet worlds in my kitchen. First there's the silence of traffic when the creepy beams of headlights come to life on my wall via Venetian blinds to conjure up nervous musings. Who's behind the wheel? Where are they going at 3 am? There's the silence of yesterday, when you run through the puzzle piece memories of another forgotten day and put another whisky bottle in the bin to be recycled. It's not even that the days are forgotten, just lacking anything worth remembering.

There's the silence of voices that used to be here— voices that were first here to comfort, and later to confront and correct. At first they were all timid about it, knowing that I needed my time, and that I had certain entitlements, that healing was a process and each grief is dealt with differently. But soon all the voices conspired together and took coin after coin out of the pity panhandling dish they were once so eager to fill. Now they are just another sort of silence.

There's the silence of Dr. Beatriz because I don't want anything fixed by a therapist whose livelihood depends on people having issues.

There's the silence of things not getting done. The world is domineering and I don't know how I ever did it all. I would have no problem brushing my teeth three times a day, could easily remember to clip my nails, brush my hair, and even shower daily, if this wasn't coupled with the implausibility of doing everything else simultaneously. If you forget to take out the garbage on Tuesday, you'll have it for another week. Unclipped nails are a sign of idle hands and the devil will use those hands to touch you at night. If you remember to use shampoo, it will run out, always before the conditioner, and then what? Who remembers to take daily vitamins daily or pay their bills on time or renew their insurance or file their taxes? Fish need food, plants water, and toilets plungers. And your bathroom sure as hell needs toilet paper after you run out of coffee filters. No one is allowed to exist without a thousand footnotes.

There's the silence of my mom, who at 3 AM is not calling me, leaving worried voicemails that end with her love and assurance that she's praying for me. If she's awake this late, she's reciting the rosary, trying to sleep. Bars are closed and not an option. It's too late and too early to do anything. It's too late to think about what to do with my useless liberal arts degree and too early to do anything with it. And this is the peaceful silence of powerlessness.

What I've learned from all these silences is there's only one silence really worth listening for: the silence of voices that are gone—the overarching silence that makes me nostalgic for the night. Not because the day unclothes any hope of hiding from this absurd nudity of brightness that strips me daily as everyone watches. Not because the stars are so great or the moon so bright. I'm not nostalgic for melancholy, or sighing romantic reminiscences, but because it is only in dark, dreamless sleep that my pain dulls enough to touch

CHAPTER THREE

Dammit. My Internet browser keeps crashing. The pop-up window tells me that "An unexpected error has occurred." I'm glad it wasn't planned. Mark used to remedy these issues with his computer savvy. But I don't need him. I only need the restart button. After a reboot, the problem goes away. Maybe there's a way for people to do this too.

The moment I connect, a chat window from Quay invades my screen. He does this all the time. Usually, I just ignore him, but I'm out of whiskey, and not even Youtube or pornography can hold my attention today.

Quay Rocky Mountain Man says: Hey bruve.

Liam says: What's up?

Quay Rocky Mountain Man says: Not too much… just saving the world, hustling and bustling, chillin' like a villain.

Liam says: We in America salute you.

Quay Rocky Mountain Man says: My tan is out of control.

Liam says: I recommend Aloe Vera gel.

All chats with Quay lead to the declaring, "Come to Guatemala!" Sometimes he uses ten exclamation points at a time and all the wildest emojis. We have nothing to talk about, so he tells me things about his life that I don't care about. Going to a place I can't find on the map is not something that I'm going to do because someone I've lost touch with tells me over the Internet. After Quay flunked out of community college he moved to NYC and a few years later started traveling. A few years ago he got back in touch with me. Since then every few weeks my inbox receives a mass email update about his life I have no interest in. I mark these emails as spam and don't even know how he got my email.

Liam says: How's it going in Africa?

Quay Rocky Mountain Man says: I'll assume that's a joke. Did you read my last update?

Liam says: Never really liked geography or reading class.

Quay Rocky Mountain Man says: It's going awesome in NOT Africa. I don't know why you aren't here… my couch is your casa whenever you decide to man up and buy a plane ticket. Quit your job and come on down.

Liam says: You'll be thrilled to know I have 0 jobs. My only job today is to remember to drink water. And I need Pedialyte but leaving the house to get it feels oppressive.

Then he asks the one question that I am over people asking me:

Quay Rocky Mountain Man says: So what's up with you?

I stand up and walk away from my computer. CRACK. I stop. Something has broken. Beneath my barefoot are the shards of what used to be a DVD. I sit back down and type what people want to hear.

Liam says: You know, not much. Still looking for a job. College wasn't as advertised. Apparently, you can't just walk into an office with your diploma and expect them to give you a bag of money.

Quay Rocky Mountain Man says: Yeah? I went to college once. . . for a few months.

Liam says: We all remember your valiant attempt to fulfill the great expectations.

Quay Rocky Mountain Man says: I liked the girls. That kept me a month longer than I would have otherwise stayed.

Liam says: I can't argue with that.

Quay Rocky Mountain Man says: So what kind of job are you looking for?

Liam says: Lots of money, very little work. The usual.

Quay Rocky Mountain Man says: Any luck?

Liam says: If by "luck" you mean someone coming to my door to offer me a job, so far no dice.

Quay Rocky Mountain Man says: I c

Liam says: You have to actually look for something to find it.

Quay Rocky Mountain Man says: That deep dude—now I need a joint.
...
...
Quay Rocky Mountain Man says: Come visit me.
...
...
Liam says: Sure.

Quay Rocky Mountain Man says: I'm mean it. Come visit me...

Liam says: What's more credit card debt, hey?

Quay Rocky Mountain Man says: Metaphysical

Liam says: Like everything...

Quay Rocky Mountain Man says: Don't use ellipsis points with me... I don't just say this to make casual conversation. Sometimes it's good to look at things from far away. I'll help you arrange the travel stuff if that's what's worrying you... I'll even pick you up from the airport and buy you ice cream.

Liam says: I don't go anywhere unless I am 90% sure there will be ice cream.

Quay Rocky Mountain Man says: Go look at yourself dude, you're young and healthy, but one day you'll be old and fat and probably bald and wrinkly and you'll finally have the money to do things that your age and kids and angry wife will prevent you from doing.

Liam says: (:

Quay Rocky Mountain Man says: Consider it... seriously consider it or I will punch you in your smiley face.

Rabble   Rabble   Rabble

I never realized how great it would be to have an apartment to myself. All of my life I have shared a house, a dorm room, or an apartment with others, and it's no wonder there was never peace. I'm finally free from Mark's nagging and Heather's glare. I can watch whatever I want on TV. I can put my dirty underwear on the coffee table, blow my nose on the curtains, and pee out the window. I've been waiting my whole life to pee out the window, any window. It's awkward because I live in the basement, but with the right angle and practice, I'll become a master. Starting today everything is on my terms. I can pee out the window while simultaneously blowing my nose on the curtains and I may be the first person in the world to ever attempt this.

With no one around to judge, I can finally get my life back on track. I'll get a job, make new, non-douche-bag friends, get a girlfriend. This is what I want.

This silence is what I want. It's different from the silences that preceded it. Before it was quiet because Mark stopped coming around. But this quiet is final. Finito. It is pure, uninterrupted silence. There will not be noise until I go out and bring noise through my door.

Mark suggested we'd still hang out. But we won't. When exactly are we going to do this? Is he going to call me? Am I supposed to, like, call him? We haven't "hung out" in months. I am free of everyone by choice. Here I am in my Zen. I will meditate every day and start jogging again. He can go get married, have kids, and wear suits and go to the gym and finish law school to become another suit-wearing lawyer—everything I don't want.

There's a lot on TV today. Hundreds of channels to choose from. I walk to the kitchen and open my fridge. What sort of meal could I make with seven expired condiments? I will ask Google. They stare out at me from their cold world. The ranch dressing looks especially forlorn sitting alone on the top shelf—cap-less, with a khaki-colored crust around its spout. In the freezer I dig away at the ice coating the walls to feel the freeze melt into moisture and pretend that the pit in my stomach is a plea for a burrito and not some inner voice making my heart sink just a little bit deeper as its beat breaks. There is not a drop of alcohol in this entire house. Not anywhere. Not even under the sink where there's always a forgotten bottle or two. Nothing. Not even rubbing alcohol. And I don't even know how to get more without shoplifting. My last credit card stopped working last week and rent is due on...

... whenever rent is due.

I need a reboot. Uninterrupted, what will I look like in another year? Are these the first steps to snowballing into a person that is not me? This is not me. I am not me.

There is a means to money, but it's something that I'll never do. It seems like I'm always deliberating, on the cusp of something. Money—it's always what everything is always about. Money is a job or doing something that will break me. But I can't work now. So I just need to sell his car. I Google plane tickets to a place I still couldn't find on a map—somewhere in the mess of all those little countries south of Mexico. Then I walk into the building's laundry room where my bike is chained to a grey pipe. When I remember the combination's last number, the lock snaps free.

Rabble   Rabble   Rabble

CHAPTER FOUR

It's never sunny in Eugene, always about to rain or just after a shower. It's cold, but never cold enough to make you put on clothes warm enough to be effective against the chill. A bike-born wind sharpens the teeth of the chill's bite and my fingers become like the cold metal beneath them. I can picture her already, wondering why I won't answer my phone.

Last week I hid like a little kid beneath my covers while she banged on my door. That's probably not normal behavior for any age. But if I can make it through the next half-hour, I'll have what I need to get out of here. It's an adorable little blue house with two stories and a mailbox endearingly made from a breadbox on an overgrown lawn. We used to celebrate Christmas right here and this is where I turned all different ages with cake on my face and a colorful cone on my head. The yard looks rural now. No one has cut the grass all year. The community beautification committee is probably going giraffe shit about it, but I bet they are afraid to say anything. Why doesn't she just hire someone to mow.

The red brick trail doesn't lead straight to the front door but weaves wastefully through the jungle lawn, past a barren plot that was once a little garden, along a little brook where water might still flow were it plugged in.

Last Christmas' wreath clings lifelessly to the front door, evidence of...

...what?

I touch the handle and ease the door open. The hinges sing from the doorframe. At the noise, my mom almost falls down the stairs to meet me in the entryway.

"It's you!" she says. Of course it's me, I've failed in my attempts to be someone else.

"Yeah. I figured I'd stop by."

"I've been calling you every day for like a month. It's inconsiderate for a son to ignore his mother's calls" She uncrosses and recrosses her arms.

"Nice to see you too?"

"Well, come on Liam."

"I'm sorry. I've just been busy looking for a job and helping Mark move—"

"Any luck?" She still stands at the bottom of the stairs.

"I have a sociology degree. I'm qualified for flipping burgers or going to grad school."

"Are you still thinking about going to grad school?"

"Yes," I say like it's just occurred to me that I could.

"Well if you are you need to start applying. Have you taken the GRE?"

"I don't mean now."

"Did you see the lawn? You told me don't hire Dan. You said, 'I'm going to mow for you.' Can you imagine what the neighbors think?"

"I'll do it. I've just been so busy with trying to find a job and stuff."

"I don't ask you for anything. It only takes a couple of hours to mow a lawn. How are you living? Can't you at least go back to bartending in the meantime?"

"I know what I need to do!"

"How are you paying for things? Do you need money?"

"No, I'm fine, I have enough still. About the car; it's mine, right?"

For a decade of my childhood, my father labored to restore a "1965 Austin-Healey 3000 MkIII BJ8 convertible." He "invested" in it when my mom was pregnant with Chris thinking it was something that he and "his boys" could work on. Despite our many differences, the one thing Chris and I always agreed on was that anything beats sitting in a dark, oily garage all day on a Sunday working on a car.

So every Sunday afternoon he'd go to the garage by himself to do who knows what to that car. Whenever anyone entered the garage, he'd look up from whatever he was doing with a greasy grin, looking embarrassed to have chosen a beautiful Sunday amongst the grime.

At dinner, he'd go into detail about what he'd done that day. "Got all the rust scraped off the fender and thinking it's finally time to gut out the interior." We'd eat what my mom had cooked and politely not listen to whatever he was saying.

"Of course it's still yours." My mom's voice interrupts my daydream.

"We need to get rid of it. We need to sell that thing, Mom."

"Do you know how many hours...years...you want to... You can't."

"Mom, it just sits in the garage."

The silence between us hides what we don't know how to say. The only thing that terrifies us more than keeping the car is getting rid of it. But the silence goes even deeper than that. It's the third and fourth person in the room with us, two immense walls of silence whose unrelenting argument shuts us both up. We are strangers who have no idea how to go further than "hello how are you?"

There's no safe place for my eyes to rest. Ghosts haunt every inch of the wall. Every photo jumps out like a masked villain in a haunted house—depraved faces grasping for fear. Who is that family? Who are they? What are they smiling about and why does happiness ooze from my dad's mouth in every one of them? Maybe that was the problem. He let all of his happiness out of his smile, and when it had all escaped, he went into the garage and never came out.

She's looking at me from the corner of her eye. "Lee, I want you to do whatever you want."

"If you don't want me to, I won't, mom."

But some change has fallen over her. There's some new lightness in her. It's as if whatever thoughts crowded her mind moments ago have left and a whole new world of possibilities has opened. She turns to me and for the first time in I don't know when she smiles, exhaling as she does, "Lee, I don't just mean about selling the car that's just taking up perfectly good storage space. I mean, I want you to do whatever you want, and the sooner you start doing it, the better."

Part II
Three Weeks Later
CHAPTER FIVE

"No—" I slap two sets of hands away from my suitcase as the big problem is eclipsed by a smaller issue of being accosted by questions I cannot answer.

"Taxi?"

"Antigua?"

"Hotel?"

I hold onto my suitcase and through it feel anchored to some semblance of an ordered reality. The internet no longer lives in my phone so there's no way to message Quay who said he would be here but is not. Every task that could rescue me seems too heavy to lift. Finding WiFi, connecting to Wifi—it would be easier just to start over, to disappear into a taxi, into a big city like diving into the ocean at night. And that's when I see it, how small everything has really been—that the things that have been crushing me were only thoughts I couldn't shake from my head.

"Hotel!"

"You need a shuttle for Antigua?"

"Taxi?"

Standing and staring in the underground street makes all the taxi drivers and hotel touts around me very uncomfortable—because, after a moment of accepting my no, they approach and venture again, "Taxi, sir? Dónde?"

It's so very clear to them I don't belong waiting on the road—life would be much better if I were in a taxi. I was afraid of this very thing. Everyone asking is a foot shorter than me, but their wills are stronger than mine, and mine is weakening. One leg wants me to go back into the airport and catch a flight home. Quay is nowhere. I predicted this would happen.

"Taxi, sir?"

"You need a taxi"

"Sir, you need taxi!"

"No, gracias. Sorry, I'm supposed to meet someone I…" I look for my name on the signs parading above the crowd.

Tod Johnson, no. Mark Maguire, no. Mark Maguire? Must be

a different Mark Maguire. Luis Marroquin, no. Dominique Santos, no. Could it be thee Mark Maguire?

"Don't touch!" Another man tries to grab my suitcase. Through language and culture, I can hear his thoughts: Get this man a taxi! He's just standing here wasting all the air.

The prices for taxis continue to get more special and then I see my name: Liam Ryan. I walk up to the little man half my height and everyone around me seems to watch, hoping I give up this charade and get in a taxi where I belong.

"I am he," I tell the man holding the sign, not sure why I am talking like English is my second language. He looks as relieved as I feel.

He's wearing black dress pants and a purple polo.

"Ah yes, Liam! So glad to meet you," he grabs one of my arms with both hands, "I am Pablo. I am here because…the…Quay. He cannot come. I am his friend. You ready we go?"

"Where's Quay," I say, not making a move either way.

"Had so much work, so sends me."

Pushing aside a large plate of dark imaginings, I gesture for him to lead the way and we walk to an underground parking garage filled with cars and motorcycles, the sad smell of concrete and oil under darkened lights—the perfect place for crime. We stop at a little motorcycle that looks like it should be parked in a junkyard. Pablo kicks it several times before it reluctantly shakes to life.

I point to my suitcase, "How will we get this on there?"

"Easy. You hold." Pablo makes a hugging motion, showing me the shape my arms will take when I hold it.

"No, it won't work. Too big."

Pablo laughs as one does at kid nonsense, "Yes, will work. Must work!"

He smacks the torn leather seat, "Going to work!"

I stand back and study the dilapidated piece of Asian machinery trembling in front of me. "Have you done this before?"

"Yes!"

"On this motorcycle?"

"On this motorcycle!"

He makes the hugging gesture again. Whatever. We'll find out soon enough. I get on the bike and we almost crash left, then we almost crash right, then we straighten and are almost struck by a van trying to also exit the parking garage. Then we shift gears and hit daylight, bright blue sky daylight in a place I try to face from my precarious position on the motorbike, one hand clutching the suitcase on my lap, my backpack pulling back, the other arm clasped around a man I don't know because he held a sign with my name on it. I envision myself flying off the back of the motorcycle, my head smashing into the pavement, a circle of Guatemalans crowding around to see the dead American. Mothers think it is horrible, but kids point and hold a sacred awe.

Look, mom! A dead gringo.

Don't look at it!

Pablo squeezes the throttle and the engine screams. I am awake to the mission of self-preservation. We are Siamese twins, connected by a black suitcase, cruising absurdly past people I never counted on knowing or seeing, rushing through cinderblock neighborhoods painted faded primary colors, unknown words printed on the side.

I guess I expected Guatemala to look like something I'd seen on National Geographic. I expected the jungle, but so far it's one giant advertisement—an urban dystopian jungle of corporate interests selling the fixes for all legal desires. McDonald's, Burger King, Taco Bell, more McDonald's, Wendys, Pizza Hut, Dominos, a giant chicken spreading a 40-foot neon wingspan. Behind him are concrete rooms stacked on concrete rooms atop concrete rooms. One building has Reconocido written largely. Recondo, pops into my mind—Latin for store. Almost nothing of my two years of Latin remains. But if Reconocido means store, then those two years were worth it.

I shout to Pablo, "DOES RECONOCIDO MEAN STORE?"

"WHAT?"

"DOES RECONOCIDO MEAN STORE!"

"WHAT!" Pablo downshifts and turns to shout over his shoulder.

"NEVER MIND!" I point to the road ahead.

"WHAT!"

"I SAID NEVER MIND!"

He turns his head anxiously around. We cruise past women balancing large loads on their heads. Children are walking behind these women carrying wood.

"I DON'T UNDERSTAND YOU!"

"I! SAID! NEVER! MIND!"

"ASK ME LATER!"

"I WILL!"

"ASK ME LATER BECAUSE I DON'T UNDERSTAND YOU!"

Guatemala City breezes by like a parade of unlikely images and then yields to a mountainous green countryside. The green hills are dotted with homes and buildings and shacks. Out of the chaos of the capital, a simplicity emerges from the landscape. Billboards advertise in English various restaurants and services offered in Antigua. I did not expect it to be like this, but I did not expect it to be like anything.

From these green hills, we enter Antigua where everything is transfigured again. A peaceful bustle spreads like a smile across cobblestone streets that cause my bag to crash into me, a final strain from as uncomfortable an hour as could be conjured. I will never be able to avenge myself against the lifeless physical objects that make existence less bearable. Somehow the present feels far away. Like it's already slipped into the past. It's like I catch some glimpse of myself a month from now, and wonder who that person is.

Pablo stops in Antigua's Central Park. We disembark and he smiles, looking satisfied. He leaves the motorcycle at the side of the street and arranges for a man to watch both it and my bag. Pablo takes out a bungee cord and lashes my bag to the bike. Pablo points to him, "It's okay. He will...watch the bike... No problema."

I eye my bag and the man. He is disabled enough that he would not get far with my bag.

"You like it?" Pablo looks from me to my line of sight. "I show you the central park...in Spanish called El Parque Central... then we go to Quay's house...It is okay?"

"Sí," I say looking about. I find the reference point for what I learned from last-minute Googling before leaving. A few blogs unimaginatively described the city as "magical." But I see what they meant. There's a small mass of people drifting leisurely from here to there, others are simply present, fixtures in the scenery, in no hurry to go anywhere.

Only two people for a thousand miles in every direction know my name. Everything seems possible when you're no one, when you haven't been fit into some form, some estimation that always feels like a miscalculation. Nothing matters, so everything is important, or irrelevant, but still might to be.

Pablo watches me with a smile while I appraise the city's central square. He follows my line of sight and says, "Antigua is," his voice trails off. "You must understand...Antigua is a very old city. And we have...history to understand...and you have to understand the city to...understand the culture in the city...the culture...it was the culture that made the city.

I hear a smattering of languages like uncracked codes and strain to hear cues in the tones.

Pablo says to look and I see the central fountain, water flowing from a stone woman's breast, and I remember the first time my dad took me and my brother to a river to swim. And I want to strip naked like the stone woman and jump in the fountain, relaxing off the afternoon heat, impervious to judgments and glances. The city is scented with diesel and tortillas and car exhaust and flowers and plants and people richly perfumed and horseshit.

I remember to imagine the coming days, that another blog said would be shaped by corrupt politicians and honest farmers and the tectonic plates of uncertain geology and mudslides and Christianity mixed with Mayan gods still breathing prehistoric breath and outside influences.

A horse trots next to a Toyota. and it's like a flash of some incoherent visions of forgotten truths. I hear a Mayan dialect from a woman in a bright weave selling necklaces, speaking to a woman dressed the same selling cigarettes.

I ask Pablo how he feels about so many tourists. He tells me that they are nice. Kind. They give to the beggars. Some are not nice, but most are. They spend money. "And your friend, Quay...he makes me ashamed. It is all foreigners like you that do the help. We who can...don't help our own people."

Kids are selling colorful candies and trinkets in tourist English.

"You buy, sir?"

"You buy?"

A kid shining a shoe watches a man holding his wife, watching a girl, watching a butterfly, pollinating the flowers. The sights and sounds and smells bang out loud the bustling beauty of Antigua. I'd read online tourists are robbed. I read the country has an undercurrent of drug trafficking and gangs. But I just see the flowers in the park's garden. I see smiles blooming and hear the fountain bubbling in the center of the park, street dogs drinking from the water springing out of the breasts of stone women who watch the way the cathedral on the park's east side rises upwards. What's behind these colonial facades! I picture knights with lances and medieval men and their 17th-century women, all seated down to a roast pig dinner.

There are sounds of marimbas and maracas, sounds that seem to agree with the bright primary colors of the Mayan clothes and buildings. A little boy is held by his mother watching tourists who are taking pictures on their phones, speaking loudly, wearing shorts, finger itching for the shutter button.   I read that the king of Spain had designated Antigua Muy Noble y Muy Leal. Very noble. Very loyal. But it all came crashing down in 1773 when most of the buildings crumbled to the ground. And just like that, Spanish America's third most important city, the capital, was ordered abandoned in the same year the Americans declared themselves independent a world away.

Antigua, the city in the highlands, surrounded by our three volcanic giants—a reminder of the geological uncertainty that looms in the background of every beautiful building borrowing time—

—1717 and the city crumbled. 1773 and the city crumbled. 1979 and the city crumbled. And today, tectonic plates sleep under three sleeping, imminent volcanoes, capricious protectors: *Agua. Fuego. Acatenango.* Water! Fire! The place of the knitting needle!

"Shine shoe mister?"

Pablo points at my Adidas tennis shoes and says something in a kind, low tone to the boy who can't be more than seven years old. He's barefoot in ragged clothes and his hands are jet black.

He dashes away into the crowd and Pablo points to my shoes, "You can't shine this variety….But he want to anyways."

We buy chocolate bananas from a man standing on top of a cooler shouting something. *Chocobananas! Deliciosas!* It's him against the world. A world that doesn't seem to understand.

Pablo confirms, "He's yelling of the deliciousness of the chocolate bananas." Pablo hands a colorful bill to the man and grabs two sticks impaling a banana caked in melting chocolate. "Delicious, yes?"

"Damn, these are good. Who knew bananas possessed this potential?" The frozen bananas melt like ice cream and the chocolate covering melts off like it loathed being stuck to that banana.

"So, how you like my city? You glad you are here?" Pablo asks.

I nod because I don't have the words. This is where I want to be and I breathe in this unlikely wind that makes me feel fresh and new and smells vaguely like a barn.

Eugene is probably pouring rain right now. And freezing. It's the end of March and it was still freezing when I left. It's hard not to feel like life isn't constantly giving you the finger when you live in a city that never sees the sun. Here could be any way. Things in my life could be any way. I flew one way, and that comes with a whole different touch to it. It feels like finding a light switch in a room after searching through the fumbling dark. I am no one here, and of all things I need a break from, it's myself.

CHAPTER SIX

"He's gross," says a removed feminine voice. "Look how he sleeps with his mouth open? You ever seen a dead possum on the highway?"

"You know I never left Guatemala, why the hell would I see a dead… whatever-the-fuck-you-say on the side of the road?"

"They have possums here you know!"

I open my eyes and the two voices pause their conversation to peer at me.

"You scared him, Luis." The feminine voice smacks the stomach of the man next to her.

She turns to hover over me and waves her hand in my line of sight, "Hola, Yo soy Shannon and this is Luis and he's a dick."

"No, don't tell it to him that way," Luis pushes in front of her, "Don't listen to anything she says."

I sit up and Luis picks up my still-sleeping hand, "So nice to meet you, Liam. When Quay first tell me your name I ask him to spell it because I have never hear of it before. Lee-ahm. It's like the girl's name, Leanne, but it is for boys."

"Don't be such a dick," Shannon
walks behind a curtain hiding a bathroom.

"No, I wasn't. I'm not." He winks at me and shows the outrageously white teeth of his smile. "I'm just saying, to me, you sound like the girl name, Leanne."

"It's okay," I tell Luis, trying to slap him on the shoulder, but missing and hitting his elbow, "it is just like the girl's name. . . but for boys."

"You see, he agrees!" he yells in the direction of the curtain.

I sit up and take stock of my surroundings. My suitcase is in front of the couch I am sitting on. The last thing I remember is looking at the depressing green linoleum floor and gray cinderblock walls. I repeat on fast-forward the conversation I had with Quay before crashing into a nap on his couch. His apartment is one long hallway that has space set aside for a kitchen and a dining room/living room. Off to one side is his cinderblock bedroom. The scent of mold escapes from behind the curtain concealing the bathroom, which, on a glance, seems to be maintained with the same hygienically apathetic attitude I adopted in my last apartment.

"We're eating steaks!" Quay walks in from the kitchen to the dining room table holding a machete-like knife piercing three dripping chunks of meat. "Come to the table dudes. These bitches are ready," he says going back for more. Then as if remembering something forgotten, he walks over to me and puts his arm around me, "The dead man on my couch has risen just in time."

Pablo from the airport walks in from the kitchen carrying plates and forks. He waves timidly, "I help make the steaks with. . . El Gringo." He points to Quay.

Quay brushes a tangle of dusty blonde hair out of his eyes. "Pablo can't say my name Liam, so I've instructed him to call me El Gringo."

Pablo examines a potted plant like it was humming, and, as if on cue, we jockey to take places on plastic chairs around a teetering card table.

"So, we should all do, like, introductions so Liam knows who he's dealing with," says Shannon, launching into the story about how she has lived here for one year and speaks Spanish better than people who have lived here for two years and that she volunteers writing grants for a charity. Before she arrived here, she traveled through every Central American country. She continues to tell her story until the plate of steaks at the center of the table steals her focus. "I would've brought something to go with these steaks if you'd told me." Her glare travels from the thick slab of meat dominating her plate to El Gringo.

Quay drops his fork. "Why the hell would you eat anything but steak if there was an option of eating more steak?"

"Well, I would have been happy to bring some vegetables or something. You know I'm a vegan." She takes a reluctant bite of her steak, angered by the taste of it.

"Shannon," Quay raises his voice, "there are vegans, and there are fucking vegans! This cow's name was Pamela," he waves a fork of meat, "and Pamela had a good life. She roamed the meadows and frolicked the pastures. And Pamela died of natural causes. So it's all good. Please don't complain in front of our guest from *Los Estados Unidos.*" Quay salutes me and bites his steak like taking control of a situation. The juice streams down the corners of his mouth in vampire fashion and Luis folds his hands in prayer, "Let us all take a moment to remember Pamela, who loved life, but who is dead from suicide in her water hole…" He interrupts himself with a staccato giggle.

"Amen," Quay makes the sign of the cross and his line of sight is momentarily lost in the single window in the apartment as if searching for not yet existing words to describe the steak. Shannon mutters something and shakes her head, also looking out the window.

"Good wine," I tell Quay because I have nothing else to say.

"It's the finest, cheapest box wine in the country. My father taught me to acquire a taste for cheap wine and beer, and you will always be able to afford both." He tops off my Styrofoam cup that has subtle teeth marks around the edges that are not my own.

Quay motions with his fork to a small dog I just now notice. She puts her paws up on his knee. Luis swallows a mouthful of steak and runs his hand through his heavily gelled hair, "Not at the table. Get off, Rosy." He flicks her in the face. "Why you do this? Huh? Why you do this?"

"She's beautiful!" Shannon places Rosy on her lap and gives her the rest of her steak.

"That you allow a dog to be at the table." Luis folds his arms.

"Our dog has nine nipples," Shannon suddenly beams.

Luis shakes his head. "No, she hab eight nipples. You are counting her twinkle as a nipple."

"No, I'm not. She has nine nipples. Look." Shannon lifts the dog by its front legs to reveal her chest and begins counting each nipple. "See, no matching nipple on this side. Nine nipples."

The dog has a matter-of-fact expression as if to say, "Yep, nine nips."

Luis rebels against even the general principle. "No dog hab nine nipples! All animals hab an even number of nipples," he turns to me to whisper, "She is counting the twinkle."

"No, look, nine nipples."

Luis is moved to examine the number of nipples himself. Solemnly, slowly, he nods. "Wow...yes...she hab... yes, actually okay, she hab nine nipples and one twinkle." He runs his fingers across the nipples and then slaps the dog's vagina. "Nine nipples. But baby she is making everyone upset that she is here while we eat."

"No, she's not," Shannon sneezes, "She wants to be here. No one else cares. Do you guys care that the dog is at the table?"

Half-heartedly, Pablo and I mumble it's not an issue. Quay devours another steak, without the aid of a fork or knife, like an animal. Shannon and Luis argue about whether or not it is healthy for a dog to eat steak. I turn to Pablo who seems to have forgotten the English he knew when we met.

"So are you from this city—Antigua?"

"No," he says. "I come here for school, then after school work. More money. I'm was from a little village, then—"

Luis interrupts and tells me he is from Guatemala City. "I come to Antigua to party and find a foreign girl and all I find is her. And she parties too much and now I can never get work done."

Luis motions to Shannon, "You know I go to jail last week because of her? Yes, I go to jail because this girl here."

"You are NOT going to tell them this!" Shannon stomps her feet.

"I cannot belieeeeb I go to jail!" Luis hurls back. "We are driving last week. And she gets angry so she starts throwing things out the window and we are both so drunk and of course the police pull us over. And they see that we are drunk and she respond by yelling at the police. And the police do not like it. So the police take me to their car, and we are inside to arrange the bride—"

"The bribe. Bra-ibe," Shannon jumps in.

"Yes, so we arrange the bribe, but while we are in the negotiations, she takes a picture of the police. Can you belieeeb that? And the police are so angry that she takes a picture that they do not accept the bra-iiiiiibe and they take her phone and I go to jail man!"

Shannon taps both her feet on the floor, "And what happened in jail? Your daddy talked to the judge and got you out right away." She turns to me, "His daddy's a politician and he's just a spoiled, rich Guatemalan who gets out of everything."

Luis gulps down the rest of his wine and addresses the table. "What can I do? It is not my fault my family hab money. And it is not easy to be rich in Guatemala, because everyone is always trying to get your money."

Shannon hits him on the head. The dog jumps out of her lap and onto Quay's couch. Luis stares at Shannon who ignores him and explains to me that people like Luis and his family could make Guatemala a better country if they wanted to. She turns her shoulder when Luis starts laughing and launches into a tirade about Guatemala having an out-of-control free market system where the upper class keeps all their wealth in the family and drives down wages for the working class. A knock makes Quay jump up and rush to the door.

"Well," I say, "it doesn't sound that different from our country."

"Yeah, because our country is like Guatemala not at all," she turns from the table to face the door where Quay is handing money to a hand emerging from the darkness.
Quay continues his conversation with us from the door, "but things are deteriorating. We at least have a middle class."

"Who was that?" I ask as Quay returns to the table.

"Someone," he says, "Guatemala just needs time. The civil war ended twenty-some years ago. Lots of people come here now and they don't consider that. The States were pretty messed up after our civil war. Things take time. Later, I want to talk to you about that."

Luis shrugs, "I'm not doing nothing, but what can I do? It is the politicians that steal all the money. But the people keep electing the bad ones, so it's their fault." Luis gets a devilish look on his face, "The bad ones like my father—"

"That's the problem!" Shannon is animated again, "It's rich Guatemalans that own everything and want to keep a cheap labor force! There are no good politicians because of people like your dad." She blows a kiss seductively towards him.

Luis crosses his arms and smiles. "It is not my fault. It is America's fault for making a mess. You cause the civil war when your CIA kill our president," he nods to Shannon.

In the rare pause, Pablo tries to say something but stops when Quay forks the last steak from the center of the table and declares, "You're looking at the big picture. You can't look at the big picture. When you look at all the problems in the world, it's impossible." He turns his head to me, "I'll fill you in later, but I'm starting to do more than just teach, you know. We can start to do more, we can do something real. I'm glad you came here."

I turn down the conversation and turn up my own thoughts. Here we are in our mid-twenties, with the solutions to the world's problems. It's stupid. We obviously don't understand the world if we think we know how her problems could be fixed. Everyone just repeats things we've read from wherever, and life goes on without needing to solve problems we'll never have the power to fix.

Pablo tries again to say something but is interrupted by Shannon who throws the rest of his steak at Rosy who's sitting expectantly on the couch. Luis's eyes darken. "*Qué asco!*"

Quay casts me a strange glare and lowers his voice, "Human trafficking man—forced prostitution, child labor—that's where the real bad guys are."

I feel like I should add something to the conversation, but I am not them. They have that spark of feeling certain ways about certain things and I do not.

"Yes," Pablo finally enters the conversation, "there are many problems here and everywhere...and in your country too. . ."

Luis jumps in but I raise my hand to him and say, "Let him speak."

Pablo lowers his hand and Rosy gently licks his palm. "I dream sometimes you know... I dream that with little things we can make, you know, the big changes. The little things that are not expected to solve the big problems. You know?"

Quay gets up and walks to the bathroom. Shannon rolls her eyes.

"Like what things?" I ask Pablo.

"Little, how do you say it? Little...inspirational things... like if there was one guitar...playing the right song to the right person... Maybe that changes the world, you know?"

Luis spits out a sip of wine and pantomimes a joint. "Let me hab some of what you are smoking, man. Yes, one guitar and one song—" Shannon pinches him silent and she reminds me of a wife reminding her husband not to swear in front of their children. Pablo returns to his silence, running his fork across his empty plate. I try to make eye contact with him in an approving way, but can't catch his gaze.

When both boxes of wine are finished, Luis balances one on his shoe and says, "It's empty." He kicks it towards Rosy to demonstrate its total emptiness. Pablo mumbles something about needing to leave to study for an English test but makes no effort to leave his chair. Somehow the topic of what I do and where I am from has not been brought up. Here I was, afraid it was looming behind every pause in the conversation. So I fill this lull with something that that ends up sounding so trite I immediately regret the words. "I really admire what you guys are doing, you know, helping people."

"I think that's what life's about, helping people. I turned down a good job in The States to come work here," says Shannon. Luis kisses her on the neck for that decision.

"And I am so happy that you came," Luis says. "What would I hab done besides have much more sex since you always have urinary tract infections?"

Shannon pulls away from him and clears the dirty dishes in a way that makes sure Luis knows she did not find his comment funny. She begins to fill up the concrete sink with water. Pablo reaches for my hand and tells me that it was his pleasure to meet me. I thank him for the ride and he lingers a few minutes before leaving. Luis offers everyone cigarettes. I decline and he and Quay walk towards the living room window to blow smoke into the night air. I look at Quay, I look around his apartment and try to understand it all. He's not who he used to be, but neither is he who I thought he'd be today. The hole on the right knee of his jeans, a faded blue jacket hanging from his cupboard, the stale pile of paperbacks in the corner, his choice of company around his table—all extensions of whoever he is. This life is all his. It is not mine. I am in the passenger seat of someone else's life.

Shannon walks over to the window and takes a cigarette from the box in Luis's front pocket. Neither acknowledges the other. She smiles at me strangely and returns to the dishes. I walk to the kitchen and fill my Styrofoam cup from a five-gallon jug of purified water a few inches from the sink where Shannon is manically scrubbing the dirty dishes. "Can I help?" I ask, even though the last dish is in her soapy hands.

"You're so harmless," she laughs, tapping my nose and

brushing up against me so that I can smell her perfume and read her intentions.

Quay and Luis have lit a second cigarette and are arguing about something in Spanish. Shannon sneezes into the dishtowel. She smiles at me strangely and points to her nose, "Do you?"

"Do I what?"

She covers one of her nostrils and inhales until I understand what drug she is pantomiming about.

"I'm afraid if I did, I'd like it too much."

"Now that's a crazy thing to say." She hands me a small vial.

"Like I said, I'd like it too much." I hand it back to her.

"If we're not here to enjoy ourselves, why are we here?"

I try hard to sound playful and but it sounds like an asshole is speaking, "Help people, right?"

"Nobody likes a martyr," she spreads a thin line on the counter.

"Everyone ready for the bar?" Quay calls from the doorway, "I gotta work tomorrow, so we need to get drunk early."

CHAPTER SEVEN

Drink 1: El Gringo yells for a round of Cuba Libres. He tells Shannon that one dollar for every drink goes to the liberation of Cuba. Shannon shakes her head. Quay insists. Shannon demurs. The bartender dodges bodies and lowers a tray of drinks from above. She stabs a hand towards me, introducing herself as Sara without an H from Israel.
"What happened to the H?" I ask.
"No one ever gave me one."
"Me either," I say, "You can have my L though. Then I'll be Iam."
"No, no. Saral sounds like something to clean toilets with." She sees an opening in the growing crowd and ducks back to the bar. We have come to the aptly named El Loco Tigre Mono, The Crazy Tiger Monkey. Quay said it's mostly expats and travelers who come here. The wooden floors seem worn from all debauchery that must transpire here. The Cubas drain and the bar crowd expands to the corners. Everything is crescendoing. Rosy is under the table. Shannon and Luis are kissing. Then they are arguing. Then hugging. Then shouting at each other. Quay clenches his fists and breaths like a maniac. Our table is in the corner next to the bathroom where an urgent flow of traffic floods by.
Antsy guy with a German accent: They let dogs in this bar?
Shannon: They let Rosy in!
Me: She has nine nipples!
Luis: No, the bar will be getting shut down because of this dog. It is against the health code.

Drink 2: After some prodding from Shannon, reminding him how rich he is, Luis orders a round of shots.
"This girl will make me a poor," he tells Sara when he hands the money.
A sticky-looking man in line for the bathroom stops us before we can down the round.
Sticky man: You can't go take the shot without a cheers!

I can't place his accent. It is very important to him that we toast to something. I raise my glass in reflex and without knowing what I'll say, declare, "To the death of our sorrows!"

There's a pause before comprehension and then six shots crash in the center of the table.

"To the nine nipples of Rosy, may she have nine puppies who will not go hungry!" Luis shouts after me.

Quay asks me something about who I keep in touch with but without waiting for my answer he darts off into the swelling mass of standing room only bodies cramming into the Irish pub in Guatemala. I am speaking to a bearded Irishman with a deep voice. He is telling me that in Zacapa, somewhere north of here, you can rent bazookas and discharge a rocket into a shed.

Drunk-bearded-Irish-man: one hundred feckin' dollars American, man. That's feckin' all it takes.

His arm washes around my shoulder as he explains the cost of renting a bazooka.

Drunk-bearded-Irish-man: But you can't just feckin' go up there alone man. In Zacapa everyone is feckin' killing everyone because the people are so feckin' bored. But I can find the hookup so you can go there and rent a rocket launcher. You get to feckin' fire it into a shed. Pretty feckin' cheap when you realize that was a rocket launcher you jist feckin' fired.

He lowers his voice and whispers into my ear.

Drunk-bearded-Irish-man: And for two-hundred dollars American, it is not unheard of to fire a bazooka into a cow.

Drink 3: Gallo Cerveza. Two Americans are waiting for the bathroom by our table.

American One: Capitalism unwitting enslaves us!

Shannon: I wanna know about all the hormones and pesticides they're putting in our food!

She picks Rosy up from the ground and pets her compulsively on the head. Rosy shakes and licks the air in front of her. Now people are shouting. Well, Shannon is shouting. She is imploding with bafflement and exploding with the rage of children engaged in a mud fight where no one is having fun anymore. Seeing the direction things abruptly took, the Americans squeeze to a different part of the bar.

Drink 4: Cuba Libres. Two girls that look too young to be in a bar begin dancing on the bar.
 A conversation by the bathroom drifts my way.
 Guy in fedora: Are you serious about coming with me?
 Swaying girl: As serious as I am drunk.
 Drone of bar: Rabble, rabble, rabble.
 Guy in fedora: Solid.

Drink 5: Whiskey coke. Where is Quay? I order a beer, to keep things light. There´s no reason to get too drunk. I empty the sugar dish and fill it with beer to give to Rosy.
 Hot chick: Is this the bathroom?
 Me: They got a pottery workshop in there.
 Hot chick: No, it's the bathroom?
 Me: No they make pottery in there!
And as quick as she could, she fled our conversation.
 Charlie Chaplin doppelganger: Can you do me a favor?
  Other person: Not unless it involves you buying me a drink.
  Charlie Chaplin doppelganger: Good, cause it involves tequila and then more tequila and after that, we start over.
 Drone of bar: Rabble, rabble, rabble, rabble. RABBLE!
 There is a dancing guy who informs everyone that if the bathroom doesn't open up in two minutes, he will pee his pants: Just look at how much ants accomplish.
 Charlie Chaplin doppelganger: Do they? Do they really accomplish anything?
 Dancing guy with a minute and a half left: Oh yes. Great big colonies.
 Charlie Chaplin Doppelgänger: But are ants happy?
 Dancing guy with one minute: Yes, very happy. All in a day's work.
 Charlie Chaplin doppelganger: No. Only the queen is allowed to have sex. And only once in her lifetime…but you can bet that that one time is better than anything a human has ever had. But then life must just go downhill from there.
 Quay: I'll be right back.
 Liam: Where are you going again?
 Quay: I'll be right back.
 Dancing guy with less than a minute: Wow, you know a lot about ants.

Charlie Chaplin doppelganger: I had colony when I was a kid. Why don't you just go pee outside?

Dancing guy with barely any time left: I always wanted one. I didn't know it was such an emergency till too late.

Charlie Chaplin doppelganger: One day...

Quay has reappeared. He grabs my shoulder and swings me around.

Quay: There's a problem.

Liam: What's wrong?

Quay: I'll be back in five.

Conversation coming from behind me: I'm not criticizing you Liz—I just think you shouldn't grab arms of people you don't know.

Shannon: Where the hell is Quay?

Drink 6: Cuba Libre and a shot of tequila. I'm in my Zen. The perfect stage of intoxication when I understand songs. American classics are blaring through crackling speakers, and each one takes me on its journey, conjures up memories made to their melodies.

Luis is saying something to me, waving his hands, but I hear only Paul.

Me: I can't hear you. This song, dude. This song...

I like, get Paul Simon. The beginning is hopeful. That's the way Paul wants it to be. Du, dut dut dut. It's simple and clear, real and worthwhile. Just a man walking down street wondering why he is soft in the middle. Why does his heart still beat with sympathy after walking barefoot on burning pavement? Is it too much to ask for a photo opportunity? Or a shot of redemption? Who would want to end up a cartoon in a cartoon graveyard?

Luis asks where Shannon is. I look for her. Quay is still gone.

Luis: Where are Shannon and Quay?

Me singing: Who will be my role model now that my role model is gone?

Luis: I think something has happened.

Luis spits and I offer a hand to a girl waiting for the bathroom and we dance. She says yes because no one can resist Paul Simon. We move to Paul's beats, swooning across the bar.

Guy on bar stool: You bump into me one more time!

She spins like a ballerina.
Dancing girl: Don't make me so dizzy!
She twists and twists and spins her polished skin shimmering off the orange light.
Dancing girl: I need to go vomit.
Paul Simon: I can call you Betty, Betty when you call me.
Drone of Bar: Rabble! Rabble! Rabble!
Paul Simon: You can call me Al!
People have made a circle around us to watch our mad dance skills.
Asshole who shoves me: There's no room for this in here.
And then the song ends, the girl goes to the bathroom, and it is time to order another drink. But I am a new man. Maybe. Just maybe the song and its moment have attached themselves enduringly to my being.

Drink 7: Whisky coke. There's always a girl. On any rum, tequila, beer, and whisky night, in an overflowing bar, the sober world outside, this world inside, music, and there's always a girl. There's always a girl whose eyes you catch from across the sea of bland faces and turns herself into the only person you can imagine building a future with. And somehow I swear I know this girl. It's not because I'm drunk, I've seen her before. She walks into the bar in a sky blue sundress with tie-dyed blotches of white clouds. I've seen these freckles and timid red lips that seem to form a practiced smile. Her sun blonde hair with a single braid mingles with the other rowdy strands of hair and wakes the nervous snake who lives in my stomach.
Liam: I know her…
Drone of bar: Rabble, Rabble, Rabble.
Luis is back, swaying at my side.
Luis: What?
Drone of bar: Rabble! Rabble! Rabble!
"Who's she, over there."
Luis: I go to find Shannon.
There is something intimate about her—like the past has tripped over the future. Everything that's not her has faded. She glows. A table has just cleared up and she sits down alone, smiling at no one in particular. She's smiling at us, at the bar—

happy that we can exist—happy that all this rabble-rousing can exist in places like this, in countries like this, in a world like this.
    Quay has replaced Luis.
    Me: Luis is looking for Shannon.
    Quay: I bet she's in the bathroom.
    He follows my line of sight to the girl.
    Quay: Careful, a scorpion that one.

It's like when you see a cat, and suddenly remember that last night you dreamt about a cat. But I can't explain these things to Quay. A guy approaches her, and leans over into her ear. She nods and he takes one of the stools away from the table.
    Luis sees me and shouts, asking again if I've seen Shannon? "Check the bathroom," I yell back.
    El Gringo stands up: But tonight is about you, so if that's the one you want, let's go talk to her.
    I put my hand on his shoulder and push him down: What? No. We can't talk to her.
    El Gringo: Oh I bet we're capable of it—you just make out the sounds of the thoughts and they listen and say stuff and boom, talking.

Drink 8: Whiskey coke. I order at the table but don't wait for it to arrive. Luis is yelling something at us from the bathroom, Quay stands on his toes and I take the opportunity to get away from him and walk towards her. On my last glance I see Shannon looks like hell and is crying while Luis holds her head, making amends for something. They take their entreating discussion outside.
    She's looking into her glass, swirling ice with her straw. A Guatemalan girl stops me as I walk over there. She grabs my hand and tells me her name. Any other time this would be awesome. I blow her off and make my jumbled way through people that I have stepped on their feet and over to her.
    "Is anyone sitting here?" Right when I say this I think of a better line I could have said. I could have walked up and looked into the glass she is twirling and said, "Looking for a friend in there?" No. That would have been worse.
    She looks up, "Go for it."
    I sit down.
    "Oh, I thought you just wanted the chair."

"And to sit here on it with you—"

"Is that so?" she crosses her arms, "You're drunk."

"I'm obviously not drunk; I am using semi-colons when I talk; I couldn't do that drunk."

"That doesn't mean that you are sober. It just means you went to college. You're absolutely smashed."

"Do you need me to stand on my head to prove I'm not drunk?"

"I'm not insinuating you aren't a talented drunk man."

"You know I have one of those faces," she says, "People swear they've seen me somewhere."

My brain is clogged and I am in my Zen—her words like a prophecy come to pass and I am suddenly so very drunk.

"Can I get you a drink?" I hiccup.

"You could never buy me enough."

"How many do you want?"

"A hundred thousand."

I shout to Sara, "Sara get me a hundred thousand Cuba libres for me and the lady."

In a flash Sara is at our side. She drops off the Cuba for me and hands this dream of a woman a glass of liquor, "Jack, right Stella?"

She downs the half-full glass and flicks her fingers into a pistol, "Adíos."

"Hey," I say, because what can you say?

She gets up and walks away and only then do I know that I got it all wrong, that of all the words I could have said, I used the wrong ones. Lucky for me, there are hundreds of bottles filled with booze and you can have from any bottle you want. Just ask, pay, and it's yours.

Drink who fucking knows: Rosy is howling from somewhere over the music. Girls are dancing on the bar. Luis pushes his way through everyone, even shoving me aside. Quay is pounding on the bathroom door, yelling something to someone —some crescendoing drama that seems further from me as it intensifies. Two Guatemalan girls pull me to dance with them on top of the bar. People can't complain because they should have moved their drinks. If they had, I would not have accidentally kicked them onto the ground and into people's faces. "Get down!" Quay shouts at me tugging at my pant leg. Something has gone wrong.

Then there is blood on a girl's nose. There are loud, concerned voices and I am swaying and when I speak I am told to shut up because this is serious, very serious. There is blood from a girl's nose. There is blood on Shannon's nose and everyone is rushing about. Then there is nothing. Then I am transported from dancing on the bar top to a taxi sitting next to Quay. Then I am back in the apartment.

Then there is nothing.

CHAPTER EIGHT

Where the knowledge of who I am and where I am is supposed to be, there is a hatchet feeling in my head. It crushes in sync with my heartbeat. The world is a dizzy place of dazing light creeping into the lonely window revealing that the day has long since dawned. I wake up because someone has shimmied open the metal door and then slams it against the cinder block doorway. A dust beam spotlights the mist of perspiration covering his face. He wipes his nose and eyes and says, "Damn, work is impossible today. Impossible. I need water. And it's only half over."

Then, like light through a window, my memory comes streaming back. I am in Guatemala. The man is Quay. My mind tries to put last night's pieces back together, but I must have drunk too much of the puzzle pieces away. I mumble a question being asked in universities across America: "What happened last night?"

Quay's face drops in the way my face used to drop when some distraction ended and I was forced to face the reality I avoided at every opportunity.

El Gringo comes back from the kitchen downing the second half of a glass of water. Fully empty, he sets it down on the plastic card table where last he served steaks and boxed wine. "Shannon," he says, "is in the hospital."

He tells me to hurry and get dressed. He only has ten minutes before he needs to be back at work.

"Walk with me," he says, "I'll give you a tour of the school where I work." He puts the word "work" in air quotes.

On the way-too-hurried walk over, Quay points out things at a rapid-fire pace. "Over that hill is where the slums are . . . well, there is one slum. . . These street dogs that always lay here, when the circus was in town they paid fifteen quetzals per street dog. For the lions . . . that bird is rare, I think. Those kids are barefoot because they don't have shoes…"

But I can't focus on much other than my body's hangover and an ongoing investigation in my thoughts as my mind endeavors to solve the puzzle of what happened last night. Muffler-less cars and trucks speed by us at unreasonable speeds.

Quay tells me that the large, trippily painted buses rattling by us are called "chicken buses." They are old school buses from The States that somehow made their way to a new life in a new world. They are painted and decorated in an absurd display of colorful opulence and followed by thick tails of diesel exhaust.

The school is housed behind a shabby, cinder block wall topped with spiraling barbed wire. Upon crossing the threshold, when you see beyond the grey outside wall, you see beauty—a place that puts your mind at ease. The school is a brightly colored pastel building surrounded by a garden of green lawns and tapestries of vines. Children's laughter erupts from every corner as kids run from one laugh to another. If there is a way to bring yourself mindfully into a moment, it is this, the abounding sound of unjaded laughter darting around a playground.

Guatemalan teachers are herding smiling pupils around. From a corner I see Pablo wave with a broom in his hand. Quay follows my eyesight and says, "Did Pablo tell you? He's the janitor here."

But the laughing kids were headed for us, and now they swarm us, attacking, grabbing at our clothes with eager smiles. They clamber to wish me good morning in a clumsy English accent. My hangover almost takes me down.

"*Hola!*" I tell them, echoing their enthusiasm.
"*Want candy! Want candy / Quay, que tal profe! / Gude morning! Want candy! / Buenos diás / Hello, how are you? / Hola! / Dulces!*"

It's a swarm of kids. Pablo walks up and turns us into a trio with a firm handshake. He doesn't say anything, just looks at Quay with a deep look of longing in his eyes that reminds me that I still don't know what happened to Shannon. A ringing bell causes Quay to grab my arm and pull me towards the school telling me, "We have to go to my classroom now."

I follow him into a room filled with kids politely sitting in front of us, controlled by a young Guatemalan woman standing in front of them, holding her hand up.

"Fourth graders," Quay whispers to me ominously, "I'm their English teacher."

"What happened to Shannon last night?"

And while I think I asked it aloud, what follows makes me

question if I did. Quay motions for me to take a seat in the back and I comply. He points to a small girl listening intensely to what her teacher is saying, "That's Rosita. They rescued her from a garbage dump. Her mom had her working there collecting plastic bottles for recycling. She weighed 30 pounds when she first showed up."

He indicates the chubby boy sitting next to Rosita, "That's Carlos. Those scars all over his body are from his mother's boyfriend. The boyfriend made the mother decide between him and Carlos. She chose her boyfriend, told her son to leave and not come back. He lived on the streets for months before one of the social workers found him and brought him here."

I drop thoughts and look at Carlos just as he says something that makes the classroom scream with laughter. The Guatemalan teacher helplessly tries to control the students with a pronounced, "Shhhhh!" Carlos basks in the bliss of having won the laughter of all 30 kids in the room.

El Gringo teaches his class like roaring thunder. Every few moments the room breaks into standing ovations at something he says. He covers the whiteboard with wild, construction-paper animals and puts on a large sombrero while pointing to objects on the board as the kids shout out answers and dance in their seats, reaching their hands toward him. His lesson ends with him lifting a boom box onto his shoulder, donning sunglasses, and hitting play as "Ice-Ice Baby" fills the room. The kids know all the words and rap with him in ridiculous accents. When the song ends Quay gets a standing ovation and takes a bow. Then he turns to the whiteboard and with great exaggeration of the phonetics says, "Okay, now we will go over the meanings of verse four. He writes across the board, So I continued to A1A Beachfront Avenue. He circles Beachfront Avenue, "Beachfront Avenue es un Calle en California. Avenue, significa Avenida en Espanol. Dile aven-new," he pauses and two dozen voices try their best to repeat. "Aven-newww," Quay says again and the kids repeat.

Next Quay draws a stick figure woman well endowed with large bosoms El Gringo colors a red bikini over and writes, "Girls were hot wearing less than bikinis." The class continues like this until key vocabulary from verse four of Ice Ice Baby has been defined and repeated.

When English class ends, it's like watching a rockstar

walking the red carpet to his limousine. The kids won't let him leave the room until everyone gets a hug or high five from him. The Guatemalan teacher laughs and pats Quay on the shoulder as he motions for me to exit with him.

Outside in the sunlight, all I can say is, "You rocked that English lesson."

"Eh," he shrugs, "I want to go out with a bang. I'm not gonna be doing this for much longer. This is just step one. . . I have ideas. . . ways to help people." He looks at his wrist, "I have an hour or so before my next class. Let's get out of here."

We exit and start walking back towards Quay's apartment.

"Quay, what happened to Shannon?" I finally say.

"She's in the hospital."

"And?"

"And I don't know, man. That's all I know. Luis only knew how to say what was wrong with her in Spanish, and I didn't know what the heck he was saying."

"I thought you spoke Spanish?"

"I do, I do. . . just not, medical Spanish."

"Why don't you go to the hospital?"

"I can't. I'm not so good at attendance here, and they've warned me. I mean I would have gone last night if I had known it was this bad. I thought she just had a bloody nose from the. . . well, I don't know if you knew but she was using blanco last night?"

"I get the impression you all were."

"Luis called me this morning. Told me what had happened. I guess when she disappeared from the bar she went to the park to buy cocaine from a guy in the park. You never buy cocaine from guys in the street, who doesn't know that?"

"Someone addicted to cocaine?"

"She's not addicted, just, work hard, play hard, that's how it's done around here. So surprise surprise, the guy didn't sell her cocaine."

"Has someone contacted her parents?"

Quay looks distantly into the unknown. "I guess I don't know how you'd even do that, maybe we could find them on Facebook or something." Then his eyes tighten on me and he laughs, "You look like shit you know."

"I hope so. I drank enough."

"You shouldn't drink that much."

"Thanks, mom."

"You aren't in Kansas anymore."

"I never was."

"Well, just take it easy and don't get so drunk until you know what's what here. I don't want to have to call your parents if you get your ass in trouble."

"Parent," I end the conversation by suggesting I might bring up that toxic topic.

Quay's skinnier than I remember. The crewcut he used to wear has been overtaken by eight sun-bleached inches of what would be primo real-estate for a rat nest. His eyes ever burning in rebellion— unsteady eyes, with a flash of danger, like a warning. I can't decide if those eyes are charismatic or crazy, maybe it's the same.

In high school Quay was just a guy I knew, a guy that everyone knew. I had only really spent a summer with him, and it was because we were forced to. We both worked at the same car wash. After that our lives rarely intersected. Quay spent high school drifting from one clique to another when it suited him. Everyone liked him, but everyone sort of hated him too.

"Do you remember the last time we saw each other?" He asks, reading my mind.

"Graduation?"

"How could you not remember?" He says imitating a southern drawl.

"High school was ten years ago."

"Are you going to the reunion?"

"Not a chance."

He shakes his head. "Well, I remember the last time. You were smoking a cigarette the wrong way. When D-man's parents let us use their camper? Remember? You can tell me now, did you and Stacy do it?"

He bites his bottom lip and raises his eyebrows.

"Oh yeah, the camper," I'm taken back to that summer, to that incident, with that girl. "That's right, you were there?"

"Of course I was. Remember what happened when I threw that bottle of bug spray into the fire?"

I don't remember that. I barely remember that he was there, or that anyone was. After four years of trying, I had finally gotten rid of my virginity. With Stacy. I did not necessarily want it to be with her, but I needed it to be with someone. My virginity had become this embarrassing monster in my bio. Everyone in our class was on a quest to ditch it before college.

I remember a half dozen eighteen-year-olds laughed uneasily, making awkward insinuations about what could have happened. That's when I learned relief shares a wall with guilt. I felt like I should be alone, like I should be with Stacy, and like I should be with anyone but Stacy. Outside at the campfire, I drank cheap beer and talked to everyone but her. She sat on a log across the fire from me, while I feigned having a blast with my friends. But my mind was far away from there, wandering in and out of an event that was both monumental and trite. Everyone searched our eyes for guidance; certain that such a change was detectable in the way I interacted with the world. Anyone having sex with anyone mattered to everyone. Sex was new, had come out of nowhere, was exciting and forbidden by the religiously-minded half of our elders. We needed help from each other to know the question: to sex, or not to sex.

Right now Quay is looking at me with the same stare that everyone had when Stacy and I walked out of the camper almost a decade ago: he's looking for some answer to a question by how I act. He wants to know if I'm giving him a green or red light.

We pass a ginger-colored soccer field where the dust is streaked in indecipherable marks that tell the tale of an endless effort to put a ball in its place of glory. He asks me if I play soccer and I tell him that I don't yet.

"Do you like it here?" he asks, smashing a cockroach dashing in front of his shoe.

"I'm on day two. So you tell me, why are you here?"

"To help—"

"You could help people anywhere. Why are you here and not somewhere else?"

He looks at me with the awe of a kid who's been informed his hamster died—more concerned at the answer to the question "how are such things possible?" than the reality of losing his hamster.

When he doesn't answer me, I ask him an easier one: "What is going to happen to Shannon?"

"I don't think she's like, going to die or anything. She's at the hospital. I don't know her that well. I'm more friends with Luis. I know her through him."

"So call Luis then."

"Okay," he nods detachedly and grabs his phone from his pocket. He hits the screen and then disappears into his phone and Spanish I don't follow. His accent is notably awkward. He's gesturing grandly, using both hands and moving his head with the phone's mouthpiece so he can gesture while he's speaking.

After an Adíos, he puts the phone in his back pocket and turns to me. "Her sinuses are damaged and might always be, but may not always be even if they are. Whatever the Bat Hell that means."

"Bat Hell?"

"He wasn't clear. I didn't understand everything. He was speaking very quickly. But he sounded worried. Maybe we should visit him."

"Why don't we visit her?"

"We can't."

"Why?"

"Luis says her father is paying for everything and gave instructions to the doctors that no one can visit her. Especially not Luis."

"You learned all that in a 30-second conversation?"

"We were talking very quickly."

"Why wouldn't he want Luis to visit?"

"Well, he's very upset about Shannon. And he must be really hurt that Shannon's dad is forbidding him to speak her—"

"Why would he do that?"

"Because Shannon's father is clearly a douche-bag. But getting back to your other question, you know that the English teacher gig is only temporary. Soon I'm going to get started on real work—really doing stuff. I'm going to fight human~trafficking…"

He whispers the words "human trafficking," like he's hiding it from the trees. "Remember Rosita? The girl at the school. She was a trafficking victim . . . and she was rescued—" Quay trips over a loose cobblestone and bumps into a Mayan woman carrying a basket of tortillas on her head. The tortillas fall out and into a man in a suit with a scrunched face. The man jumps back and bends his knees to help the old woman up. The Scrunched Faced Man and Old Woman stand up and turn to Quay who points to the street and says something in Spanish.

The man points to the tortillas and says something. Quay

turns to me, "They think this is my fault. But I told them that shit happens. It's life's fault."

"Just pay her for her tortillas. How much could they be?"

"Occupational hazard. I'm a starving volunteer."

"Fine. I'll pay for them." I grab a wad of American dollars from my pocket and give the woman $20. This seems to solve everything. Both the man and the woman seem very happy with this arrangement. The man points to his suit and says something to Quay. Quay translates to me, "He wants to know how much you are going to pay for the damage to his suit."

"Are you kidding me? There's no damage to his suit."

"Liam, if you are going to pay this woman a week's salary because life spilled her tortillas, I think you should pay this man something for the damage done to his suit."

"No. That's crap. There's no damage."

"There's emotional damage to it."

"Shut up," I give the man a dirty look and say, "No." with a scolding finger. It does the trick and we continue walking.

"I was just kidding back there you know," Quay says. "About the suit."

Not content with silence, Quay pushes the conversation on, "What have you been up to lately?"

"Like I said in our chat, I've been doing nothing. Nothing I care to talk about at least."

I think about my last year of fuzzy, uneventful, moments bleeding into each other, void of any purpose. "Well, that's all a long way away from here. Everyone arrives here being whoever they decide to be when they get off the plane or bus . . . if you want, you can start to volunteer around here in the mornings if you aren't always hung-over."

"It was the first night," I say. "I was just welcoming myself to Antigua."

"It was quite the welcoming party."

He laughs, and I smile, but not on the inside.

"Gotta start off on the right foot," I say, losing the argument. I stop walking and look Quay straight in the eyes, "Thanks for getting me down here. I needed a change of scenery.

CHAPTER NINE

I walk through Antigua's colonial streets and amid colorful buildings that look like they've seen it all. None of the streets are marked. On some streets there are more gringos than Guatemalans. German accents, British English, Scandinavian beauties in backpacks are crossing every street. This seems more like some cosmic hippie meetup as much as one of the great colonial Latin American cities. We cast odd glances at each other, knowing neither of us really belongs here. On every block are young shoulders hauling hefty backpacks with months or years packed away inside.

A woman seated penitently on the curb looks up at me longingly. Beggars have their beats on the corners of the busier blocks. The streets are a bed and a home and where people go to work when there is no work. They extend their homelessness towards me via little cups. I am weak, so I drop a few quetzal coins in the tins and hear the resulting clink, the sound of either a good deed or the perpetuation of deep societal cuts. Some smile at me, others look up with forlorn and accusing eyes. They know it should not be like this. My mind drifts back to college classrooms, where far away from this street we discussed the world's harsh realities that were too distant to touch back then. You're only giving them fish for a day, Professor Harris would have said about my offering of alms.

Are you helping or hurting?
I'm trying.
So are they.

Back then, between smiling and scowling, nursing hangovers while nodding and agreeing and disagreeing, we solved these problems in our term papers. They had elaborate titles:

Poverty as a Function of Capitalistic Systems.
Misappropriated Charity, the Enabler of Social Inequality.

I want to help them. I don't want to establish fair trade with them or invest in the education of their children. I want to help them right now, and so I do. I cast coins in their tins and don't care what Professor Stenlich or Professor Harris or

Professor Scrooge would say. It's not as if being a few dollars up or down will change my life one way or the other.
Or their lives either.
Hush.
From Quay's list of sights to see, I navigate through the city via his hand-drawn map but quickly discover that Quay's map, like his life, is unintelligible. I buy a used Lonely Planet guidebook at a bookstore-café called El Baul. I open it and a small piece of paper falls out. One side is a list of items that seem appropriate for traveling in Guatemala: Imodium, flashlight, rechargeable batteries, memory card, baby wipes. On the other side written in capital letters: "I AM LIVING A DREAM BECAUSE OF YOU!" I look around me as if the person who wrote it must still be somewhere nearby. There are so many of these little windows we find everyday into other people's lives, most already too far removed to see past the curtains.
Armed with the manual, I rush from one site to another, looking and reading my paragraph description of it, then moving onto the next one.
Palacio de Los Capitanes, dating from 1558, the Captain-Generals' Palace was the governmental center of all Central America from Chiapas to Costa Rica until 1773. Today the palace houses offices. *Palacio de Los Capitanes*, check.
Catedral de Santiago. Begun in 1542, demolished in 1668, rebuilt between 1669 and 1680, repeatedly damaged by earthquakes, wrecked in 1773, and only partly rebuilt between 1780 and 1820.
Catedral de Santiago, Check.
Iglesia de San Francisco. Little of the original 16th century *Iglesia de San Francisco* remains, but reconstruction and restoration over the centuries have produced a handsome structure.
Iglesia de San Francisco, Check.
Iglesia y Convento de Nuestra Señora de la Merced. Three blocks from *El Parque Central*, pass beneath the *Arco de Santa Catalina*, which was built in 1694 to enable nuns to cross the street without being seen. Because being seen in the street would have surely led the nuns to fall from grace.
Rebuilt with its clock tower in the 19th century. *La Merced*'s construction began in 1548. The most recent of its several

bouts of rebuilding has taken place since the 1976 earthquake. Inside the monastery ruins is a fountain 27M in diameter—the largest in Hispanic America. It's in the shape of a water lily, the symbol of power for Mayan lords.

I face the church's bright yellow façade just as both of the twin bell towers chime. 3 p.m. There are half a dozen stone statues placed symmetrically on the portico. The largest statue of Mary with downcast eyes is above the entrance's two wooden doors built for giants. All around Mayan women in bright woven garb sell local food, children drink soft drinks from flimsy plastic bags, and tourists snap barrages of photos with their phones. I lost my phone on my first wild night and don't miss it.

Street dogs dart uneasily about from scent to scent, and pigeons fly from this to that. On the grounds in front is an enormous stone fountain. Only a few timid drops of water drip from it. Sitting on the fountain's rim is a kid with firmly gelled black hair playing a guitar and singing to an entranced girl. She's young. Maybe feeling these feelings for the first time. She's finally part of the story. Here is a princess. There is her prince armed with six strings where she can lose herself.

My eyes pan out from the fountain and there she is, the girl from my night of shattered memories. I see her sitting on a bench, throwing crumbs to pigeons. A dozen alcohol-suppressed memories from last night summersault through my mind. I had forgotten. The girl with the small braid mixed in with the rest of her hair. I remember her. I can't quite recall the content of our conversation, if it ended poorly or well, but I know what seeing her now feels like. Spring.

I walk up to her and unmagical words come out of me, "Do you remember me?"

She hurls some crumbs a bit aggressively towards the birds, "Oh, you're not one to forget. Quay's drunk friend, right?"

"You know Quay?"

"It's hard to miss the loud morons."

"We all have our moments, I suppose."

"Well, I know what you guys are planning to do and it's stupid and crazy and you can tell him I said that."

"What are we planning to do?"

"With Shannon?"

"What are you talking about?"

"Oh," she switches from lecturing to evading. "How well do you know Quay?"

"We went to high school together."

"And you know what happened to Shannon?"

"She bought some bad drugs, yeah? Was her fault, I guess."

"Well that's refreshing." She tucks an escaping strand of her yellow hair behind her ears and yawns loudly, "At least someone in this gossip town doesn't know."

"What more is there to know?"

"Well, you know the details. You got the facts. You don't want to worry about pointless gossip." The sun behind me makes her squint when she finally looks up at me, "You're sure Quay hasn't asked you?"

"Look, stop being mysterious about this, either tell me or don't."

"I choose the latter," She gets up and wipes bread crumbs off her dress and the pigeons go wild, "See you around."

"Nice to meet you again, Stella" She stops and we share a moment of eye contact, both surprised to know her name. She turns back sharply to face the squinting light. "I don't know you or owe you anything, and I am not going to feed the rumor mill that's all. This whole town is just one big gossip circuit you know. Seems like this big maze when you first get here but it's really just nine-by-nine blocks filled with a few hundred gringos who are alcoholics and assholes. That's all people do. It's why I'm not going to stick around."

And with that, she's gone. So I get up too and look up at the church and listen to my footsteps pass through the front door. On the ceiling above the entryway is a blue bust of Saint Peter. An ancient woman to my right is selling candles; next to her, an even older man sells rosaries and prayer books.

The church is an empty tavern with a long, incense perfumed nave leading pew by pew to the altar, which to the people kneeling before it leads to something further. On either side of the path between the pews are statues of various saints and Mary and Jesus; petition candles burn in front of each atop hard irregular blobs of cold wax. I stop at Saint Anthony looking desolately out over a table of candles and recall him being the patron saint of lost things.

And in front of it all is the golden tabernacle where a small red flame burns to make an incredible claim about a presence and essence. Fresh white flowers have been placed vigilantly in front of it. I wonder if my mom is prostrate in front of the same golden box thousands of miles away.

I walk up to the front and genuflect. My knees' muscle memory remembers what all this once meant to me, what it still means to my mom. How much easier things would be if I could just surrender to blind faith without the need for endless analysis of everything.

Does it matter if it's true if it makes life easier?
Drugs make life easier too.
That's different.
Only substantially.

Who is this voice always questioning things in my head? High windows let the late afternoon's magic hour inside. There are a half dozen people scattered about the pews in prayer. One woman has her eyes shut firmly, but tears force their way out down the span of her cheeks. Regardless of what I believe or what I do not believe, why would anyone ever want to take away from this woman what is keeping her eyes closed? It's giving her comfort. And then it just doesn't matter. How often have I tried to take away from my mom what she likely needs more than anything? How painful and drawn out was the process of leaving my faith behind?

But churches make me dizzy. I stand up and count my echoing footsteps. Outside I avoid eye contact with the beggars sitting out front. I've already given all my change away and there are too many to give to them all.

Iglesia y Convento de Nuestra Señora de la Merced, Check.

The light is dimming. I wanted to make it to the market, but I'll save it for another day. My last site is the Cerra de la Cruz. Overlooking Antigua from the north, it "provides fine views looking south over the city towards Volcán Agua."

My guidebook is not wrong.

Out of breath from the climb, I see Antigua with parental eyes, the city in its entirety seems tired and satisfied, like a grandparent with nothing left to prove. The smell of campfires from wood-burning stoves flavors the air with an ever-changing aroma that shifts in character. You notice it and try to remember where you've experienced the scent before. I sit down at the foot of the cement cross at the top of the hill and look below. It's quietly bustling, people making the hike to catch the sunset.

And then there's Stella again and dammit she's going to think I'm a stalker. She appears here from a road leading further up the mountain, jogging hastily down the hill, avoiding various pockets of photo-snapping tourists, she dives past me lost in the world of her iPod. I wave but she pretends not to notice.

Something about her makes me think of my brother, but I shove thoughts of him away because I don't know how to hold them and I feel the cooling evening shiver. It should be warmer this close to the equator. The light is fading fast so there's nothing left to do but find my way back to Quay's. The horizon begins to glow and the clouds mimic the colors. Hues of pink surround an orange globe that is contrasted by a darkening city. The peak of the volcano fades into the black. When it disappears completely, the hill empties. Soon it's just me and a few lingerers looking at the lights below. I make a wish and walk down the hill thinking how wishes carry the hopes we're too afraid to touch.

CHAPTER TEN

I unlock the door to Quay's cinder block apartment and enter to a half-dozen guys of various nationalities seated somberly around the table. They looked like I've interrupted their grandmother's wake. "These are some friends," Quay mumbles with wandering eyes. He itches his scalp and says, "They're friends of Shannon too, so we're talking about what happened and what we should do."

Whatever everyone is discussing has clearly been derailed by my entrance. Quay says something in Spanish to the group which makes them all glance at me. "I'm going out," I tell Quay.

He nods. "We'll talk later."

I grab my sweatshirt and head for the door I just entered. It's Wednesday night, and the streets in Antigua are fuller than yesterday. I see the bar we went to on my first night and wander inside. A wobbly man with an impressive beard enters after me and is still standing in the doorway shakily assessing the situation. Alcohol pours from his mannerisms. He shifts his weight from left to right. With a sense of awe, he looks at the half-dozen faces around the bar consumed in their own world, like he's surprised at the existence of others, like he has been in a coma for a decade and has awoken to find the whole world unrecognizable. Another puzzle piece appears from last night and I suspect he's the one who told me about renting rocket-launchers for $100 and firing them at sheds or cows.

He looks from face to face; unsure if this is the happiest moment of his life or the worst. There's a beat and he decides on elation and gleefully falls onto the stool to my left.

He seems to know me without having had to go through the demanding effort of meeting someone. "Only twenty-five dollars man, and that comes with everything."

"Twenty-five dollars?"

"Brafinakinman!" His Irish accent sinks to a deep baritone. He holds an empty hand to his face and seems surprised, shocked even. Staring long enough to ensure all fingers are still connected, he turns to the bartender "I dunt have me a beer!"

"Well, whose fault is that?" The girl behind the bar puckers her lips.

"I dunt knows. It's jus not his feckin' fault," he points to me, "He's a good shite. This man would always be makin' sure I had a beer."

"Isn't this already the end of the earth?" I ask him.

"Do you want a beer, Joes?" the bartender picks up a bottle of Gallo and swings it menacingly in his line of site.

"Yes, course I want me a Gallo. Of course! What do you think? And get one for me mate."

Pleased that I am now his mate, I accept the beer, which is probably a better idea since the rum and cokes I drank the first night were bound to lead me the wrong way down the path of righteousness. But no matter how much I drink tonight, Joes will win the prize for being the drunkest one in the bar.

"CHEERS!"

"Cheers!"

Joes coughs some of his beer back up, "Ah this Gallo is feckin' shite man. But never tell that to a Guatemalan, or he will slit your feckin' throat. They all got knives just in case someone beats on their beer. They will tell you it is the feckin' best beer in the world, because they have only had two feckin' different kinds of beer in their whole feckin' life. "

"I'll keep that in mind." Joes is either farting, or there are dead animals hidden underneath his jacket.

"You better mate, you feckin' better or…" Leaving me hanging on a conjunction, Joes lowers his head and looks serious. He stares at the bar with his eyes raised menacingly towards me. His volume remains the same, but he has taken to mumbling in order to ward off any eavesdroppers. " H e y ~ m a n ~ w h a t ~ d o ~ y o u — thinkaboutgettingsome~lassies~to~suck~our~willys?"

"In principle, I'm in favor," I say.

"Twenty-five dollars man, that's all it feckin' takes!"

"For whats?"

"Twenty-five feckin' dollars for a little sucky-sucky and they include a cigarette for feckin' free, man."

It's time to change the subject, so I ask. "Do you know Quay? Or Shannon?"

He straightens up when he hears me say this. "What do you know about Quay and Shannon?" He has a new menace in his eyes.

"I know what happened last night."

"So you know then?" he asks me, and it seems the rhetorical question sobers him.

"Yes."

"Are you going to be apart of it."

"Yes," I lie in order to get some information.

"Well, good for you, sir. I just can't you see. I can't. I support you guys. But be careful. People know about what you are planning to do. Not that you'll get caught. Murders in this country don't lead to shite, but you know what happens when people talk."

Without warning Joes rises and resumes his quest, "Twenty-five dollars man, what say you man, girls for twenty-five dollars? You won't get it better anywhere else."

Joes is finished—barely able to sit on a barstool, much less make it to the underworld to make a transaction with what I presume are prostitutes in reference.

My beer is empty and I decide to switch to a whisky coke. This is only my second and this is fine. I'm on vacation and I am tired and for once I have a reason to drink. It's 10 p.m. and there is nothing else to do. Plus I'm finding out valuable information about whatever Quay was discussing at his plastic table.

Joes' plans seem lost with the lit cigarette that fell from his mouth and turned to ash. The determination has faded from his face and his head is bobbing onto the bar. Smelling the smoke, the bartender is back in our vicinity in a flash, "Who's smoking in here?"

Wearing the guilty expression of a child who has had an accident in his pants despite being a big kid, Joes' eyes close and his head drops to the bar. I start to feel self-conscious at my proximity to him, but then remember how little any of the matters. I am anonymous here, and maybe I've always been, everywhere.

As a pair of Australian accents walk through the door, Joes' head bobs up from unconsciousness and he faces me, "Hey, do you have twenty-five dollars that I can borrow then man?" Without waiting for an answer, he gives me a wounded look and hobbles off his stool to the door. The bartender smiles, catches my laughing eyes and shakes her head at his wake.

CHAPTER ELEVEN

"Yeah, it's not a very comfortable couch, is it?" Quay sees me shifting in the early morning light. I can't decide where the pain is coming from. My body feels like a Sex Pistols song. The pain in my head is likely from last night's whisky. The pain in my feet and knees is probably from walking, which might also be where the pain in my back is from. The pains in my elbows and teeth are inexplicable.

Quay sits down on a chair and sets a mug of black coffee in front of me while he sips his own. "It's cold," I tell him, surprised.

"Yeah, it cools down at night, it surprises people sometimes."

"How did your seance go last night?" I ask, searching his eyes.

"Fine. It went fine. We spoke to Michael Jackson, and we're not sure, but we might have had Lincoln on the line." He laughs at his joke and clarifies, "they were all friends of Shannon and we were just figuring out what to do about it all."

"How is Shannon?"

"Her dad arrives soon I guess. He's in communication with a doctor in The States who's advising the doctors here and I think she's going to be flying home soon. Luis went back to Guate City, I think because her dad's here. They didn't really get along. It was worse because it took the doctors a few hours to figure out what she had taken."

"Were you all on coke?" I ask, surprised by my directness.

Quay stutters, caught off guard, "I like never do that. I told her that buying from the dealers in the park is a stupid, stupid, stupid, stupidstupidstupid idea. You CANNOT buy drugs from the guys in the park, bad shit always happens. . ." He glances at his watch and finishes his coffee in one chug.

"So what was there to talk about with those guys last night?"

"That night . . . after I sent you home in a cab, we needed to find out what Shannon had taken so the hospital could help her. If they don't know what you took, they don't know how to treat you. So we found him. The drug dealer from the park. Luis and I and two of Luis's friends and we made him tell us what he sold Shannon so that the hospital could treat her."

"You told me you didn't know it was that bad that night."

"I didn't."

"What do you mean you made him tell you?"

"Do you know what he sold to her?" Quay interrupts me before I can guess. "Fucking battery acid! He sold us oxidized battery acid. You know those white crystals that form on an old car battery? He sold that off as cocaine and it ate away at Shannon's face and her sinuses and she's forever fucked because this guy sold us battery acid."

"And the police?"

"The police?" Quay scoffs, "I don't expect you to know how stuff works here, but we're not in America. We can't just call the police and expect them to make everything better. It's the Wild West here. You either take care of things yourself or they don't get taken care of."

"What did you guys decide last night?"

I hate the way his voice wavers. "We needed to decide what to do."

"And did you?"

"We decided that this guy is not going to be allowed to hurt more people."

"I talked to Stella. . ." I say knowingly, fishing.

"The hippy girl? Everyone here cares way too much about everyone else's business. Do you know how many murders get prosecuted here?"

I shake my head.

"Less than 3%. That means that everyone literally gets away with murder here and justice is a joke."

"So what are you going to do?"

"Nothing that you'd understand after being here two days."

"I walked off that plane two days ago to take a break from my own shit. I didn't know I'd be landing in a complete shit-storm."

"I'm not disagreeing with you, this is a storm of shit my man. But we didn't cause it, we're the ones fixing it."

"If it wasn't so ridiculous, I'd think "fixing it" means murder, a word you're obviously afraid to use since you keep justifying things to me without telling me what those things are. If your friend got messed up on cocaine, then she probably knew the risks going into it, and as shitty as it ended up, she's not like an innocent victim.

"—Liam, you don't understand anything."

"No, I don't," I take a scalding swig of my coffee, "and in a way, I'm glad I don't. So enlighten me wise one. Tell me what exactly happened and what are you planning on doing about it or leave me the hell out of it."

Quay's eyes harden and soften. We can't look at each other, so we stare down the dented green linoleum below us. I'm so used to being the most screwed-up person in the room that it has not occurred to me that maybe he could use what everyone needs—a bit of compassion. I slow down my voice, "I'm not going to judge whatever it is; you can trust me."

This might even be true. I might be trustworthy—capable of guarding the secrets and withholding judgment. When both of our wandering eyes find the couch that is my bed El Gringo asks me, "Did you sleep like shit on it or what?"

"Yeah, it's not the most comfortable."

"You're welcome to stay on my couch of course, but hostels aren't expensive. There's The River Rio, just off the park, behind the cathedral. For ten bucks a night you get a bed and they include breakfast."

We both agree that my comfort is important and free breakfast is hard to pass up. He gets up and changes the subject, "Remember you're scheduled to volunteer at the project tomorrow, at nine," that's what he calls the charity he works as an English teacher for: "the project."

I change the subject, "Do you know how I can see Stella?"

His eyes blink blank at the question. A well of words surface on the ocean of his eyes, but then, as if fatigued from all the talking, he answers simply and directly, "She works at that wine and cigar shop near The Big Yellow Arch." And he walks towards his bedroom, set off across the curtained-off bathroom. He enters and closes the door behind him. Within a few minutes the memory laden aroma of cannabis perfumes the apartment's air. So that's that—two days as a passenger of

Quay's life, and now I've gained my independence and have to steer my own ship. I pack my things back into my suitcase as Quay goes to the bathroom to ready himself for work.

CHAPTER TWELVE

I rock up to The River Rio, a cheap backpacker hostel with a hallway painted bright orange on cinderblock. A Guatemalan woman is gatekeeping the front desk set perpendicular at the end of the hall that opens into the central courtyard with numbered rooms surrounding it. To get there you must get past her.

Out in the street my suitcase busted a wheel, so now I'm without a phone and dragging an oversized rectangle full of stuff I mostly don't need. Past the woman is a table of Australians drinking beers and playing cards. They lay the cards down with a certain detachment—nothing worth talking about happens in the daylight. Opposite the Aussies a sunburned blonde with brown insect bites dotting her tanned legs drapes out of a hammock. Her sunglasses stare disinterestedly at a paperback with a muscular, naked man embracing a standoffish woman on the cover. I want to enter the ranks of the likes of this crowd but first must get clearance from the robust woman who has smiled and given me a warm *buenas tardes*.

$10 a night. This is so insane. Plus breakfast? Where has this world been hiding?

The woman gets right down to business. Without asking what I want, who I am, or what I am looking for she says, "Passport please."

I rifle through my backpack and then hand it over. She jots down information and then takes me past the Australians who wave like cool kids, beyond the bug-bitten woman on the hammock who nods, and to a room with four bunk beds. Two of the four mattresses have large backpacks bleeding their contents onto the unmade sheets. I look down at my Walmart suitcase. I'm an outsider in this world of nomadic backpackers wandering. The carriers of these packs are the real deal. They are travelers. I've only traveled here. How did the world become theirs, and what do I need to do to make it mine?

I choose the free bottom bunk in the corner and kick my suitcase under. Thusly settled, I drift past the shelf of paperbacks in the hostel's book exchange. Mostly romance novels that never should have been purchased, much less written. No book capturing me, I ramble to the rooftop terrace and then stare out across the city. Below me is the city. It's all out there. Unfolding. Cars drift through the street with apparent purpose as humans ant their way across the sidewalks. I feel a voyeuristic rush at making the lives of others my spectator sport. Everyone seems like they are so capable of going about their lives as if forgetting we are hopeless specks of dust on an average planet orbiting an average sun in a typical galaxy somewhere in the universe that science spends its time figuring out how it all began. One day the sun will swell and burn up the earth it once nourished to life.

The roof has a large cement sink in one of the corners and linens hanging in the other. I hear someone walking up the stairs and turn around. The newcomer's carefree swagger goes with long, unkempt hair. He rests his hands on the wall and follows my line of sight out across the city below. He smiles and nods to the city, elated it seems. He takes a deep breath and pulls out a joint from his pocket which he lights and inhales. He sighs and his exhale is like singing a pent-up answer to the fierce unanswerable questions of life. Then he walks over and passes the joint to me.

I stare at the red hot cherry at the end of it. I am about to pass it back and explain I don't smoke, but it feels too heavy, resisting the realities that saunter towards you with such certainty. So I breathe in dank fumes that fill my lungs then mind.

"Max," he says, extending a hand.

"Liam," I tell him, accepting it. He's Israeli. I ask him about himself. Ever since he got out of the Israeli army, he has been traveling. He started in Peru and plans to travel all the way to Canada. Of all the countries, he says that Colombia has the best weed.

"Many Israeli guys go and travel after the army," he says. "It's necessary. You see so much shit in the Army." He takes a long slow drag and continues his musings with smokey breath, "But Israelis like to travel with Israelis and stay at Israeli places and eat at Israeli restaurants. It's like they leave home but stay as close to home as they can."

He passes the joint back to me and continues, "But for me I like to travel alone. Three years I carry a gun and it's a crazy power to have, to carry a gun. So I will spend three years traveling to shake all the sand and bullets off me from my time in Army. Max looks at the city with glazed eyes and is saying something that I don't understand, I am lost somewhere inside my head. I am thinking about depression. No, I am thinking about depressed people. That's the worst part of depression, is understanding that it's an illusion you could escape if you could see through it. And that's the tragedy—you can't, because it's the very thing you're lost in. Some part of you understands that the world is not bleaker than it used to be on even your most elated day. Intellectually, you comprehend that on the grand scale everything is still as intact as it was in the moment of your most fervent bliss. Yet still you lie in bed, blind to every cloaked joy. And still, you lie to yourself that this is just how things must be because holding onto your reasons is more important than remedying them. There are so many ways to see everything. There is any way to see anything.

"You never see Dinosaur penises in pictures," I tell Max, saying what could be the worst possible thing to say to an ex-Israeli soldier.

Max either doesn't understand or chooses a different path, "You want to learn how to swear in Hebrew?"

He teaches me the lyrical "*Zayn ba aye!*" A dick up your eye! Then I forget. He teaches me again. *Zayn ba ayn*!

"You say it when you don't want to do something," he says, " many Hebrew swear words are Arabic words."

I look at my shoes and realize that they're too big. My whole life I have been buying my shoes a half size too large in order to be ready for the eventual growth of my feet and when they stopped growing I was stuck buying shoes a half size too large.

We walk downstairs to the hostel's commons area. I ask the no-nonsense lady at the front desk if they sell orange juice. She looks up at me with a tired confusion—I am just another mumbling gringo.

She's lovely, in a way. Like something lost. It's not that we could not be together. Not that we could lead a blissful life together. But because love is mostly about context. It is only ever about context. I see girls in bars and on the street. I see girls sitting at the same airport gates, but they do not end up in the seat next to me. We smile politely with no reason not to love or hate. This contextual tragedy will always separate us.

Maybe I am not depressed. Maybe it's just that my expectations were higher than life could deliver.

What's Quay doing now? What's he plotting? What's he up to?

Oh no, how long have I been standing here staring at this woman? Am I staring? Shit. I am staring. Have I asked my question yet? She looks right at me, possibly through me. Max is behind me. I point to the cooler. She looks at the cooler.

"Orange juice," I say, as clearly as I can.

She opens the cooler and takes out a beer. I accept this. She seems to know of my needs better than I do. But let the record reflect, I did not want to drink alcohol so early in the day, all I wanted was orange juice.

Max tells me he needs to go to a travel agency near Central Park so that he can book a bus ticket. He is heading north. He's been in Guatemala for too long and now it is time to go to Belize. He asks me if I want to go with him and I tell him maybe. He tells me I need to decide now, so I tell him no. He pats me warmly on the shoulder and says, "*Adios amigo.*"

"Take care, man, it was crazy to meet you," I tell him. What I mean is that who the hell knew that in this world you can do things like fly across the world, meet someone from across the world, smoke pot with them, and say *adios* all within such short period of time and then they can return to a life that will never again intersect with yours.

"*Zayn ba ayn!*" I tell him as a final greeting, "A dick up your eye!"

What is this mysterious world so filled with different people's lives? And really none of these lives are really off-limits to us, we can cross paths with whomever. We can choose our own lives and use those lives to cross paths with people who make a good fit. I am so stoned, I realize, relishing the intrepid nature of these thoughts that drift to the wine shop under the arch street and Stella.

CHAPTER THIRTEEN

Walking through Antigua, things seem brighter, more imminent.

Amid the still alien hustle and bustle of Central Park, there is a group of musicians present. A marimba, a guitar, and drums. As their song assails me, I feel a sense of personal shame that I do not play a musical instrument. It should have been required when I was in school. What have I been doing with all these years that was more worthwhile than putting my soul into a song?

Four marimba mallets move magically across the instrument's wooden teeth. Below the upbeat sound of the marimba is the holistic sound of a guitar and the driving beats of bongos. There is something here—buried beneath the surface of the sound is something true. It has access to things I don't. Something is alive and coming out of it. A few locals and tourists have stopped to listen to the music. We all share it from different angles, from different lives. There is no reason that I couldn't have been them. It just turned out that I wasn't. I ended up being me through no fault or merit of my own.

The music reaches towards something; there is a longing for arrival. It pushes against a fleeting boundary of my dreamscape where even my wild imagination finds a fence. Music is this longing, a single protest against my human limitations, a protest against my spirit's inability to transcend. Maybe in all art there is this reaching. Maybe smoking pot or snorting blow is also this reaching. Maybe we run marathons to reach for this—so much longing for something beyond.

The song ends and I can't remember how long it lasted, though I feel like I've been here for a very long time. The day is hot and beads of sweat accumulate on each musician's bronze forehead. They are dressed in faded colors with long hair decorated with ribbons falling over their necklaced necks. The next song is faster than the last one, but equally as impossible, filling the air with the white colors of possibility.

I follow a little girl's finger pointing to the sky and see a kite flying overhead. The kite's bright colors are struggling to rise. The notes are struggling against the silence. It pulls in vain, rising with the music towards the lightly blued sky. It will never make it through. The same string that gives it flight will keep it forever far away from the heaven it fights for.

As if remembering who I am, I remember my mission and begin to walk towards the arch a few blocks from the park. As I near the arch, I see a small store whose walls are filled with bottles of wine and assume I've found it. Peering through the glass, someone knocks on my face. Stella is on the other side of the glass.

"Take a picture, it'll last longer," she shouts through the transparent barrier.

"Sorry," I say, walking in, "But I have a very important message. . ."

"Oh really?"

"Have you accepted Jesus Christ as your personal lord and savior?"

Her imposed grimace continues to look unimpressed with me, but underneath it, I see a smothered smile. If she didn't open her mouth, I'd think she was sweet and innocent—adorable really—the kind of person you just want to hug and hold. But her words contrast this impression. "If you don't have plans to buy some wine or cigars I'm going to have to ask you to leave. And by ask, I mean I'll make you leave."

"I moved into a hostel."

"I once owned a guinea pig named Wilbury, after The Traveling Wilburys. So what?"

"Quay's a mess. I talked to him this morning, but he was all over the place."

"That's because half the time he's cracked out of his mind. Maybe you should be more careful about who you call a friend?"

"I didn't pick him," I say.

"You don't strike me as the lynching type," she says, pantomiming a knife across her neck. It's the first time I've heard that word used. It's the correct word for what is being planned and seems much tamer, softer than a word like "murder."

"That can't be what they're planning to do. It wouldn't make sense."

"Nothing does. I just know what I hear. I heard you

met my friend Joes last night . . ."

"And you're careful about the friends you choose?"

"When you ask a question that way, you're only passing a judgment. So tell me, Liam, right?—are you buying anything then?"

I grab a bottle at random from a shelf, "This."

"Excellent choice, one of our most expensive wines. From Italy."

"What's your deal?"

She stops, affected by the question, but recovers quickly, "What's yours?"

"I don't know," I say, and I realize it's one of the things I'm most sure of in this moment—I don't know why I'm here or what to do or how to heal from what I don't even know how to face. I smile as disarmingly as I can. "You seem familiar and nothing else here really does. I'm not saying that to hit on you; I would swear I've seen you before—"

"You wouldn't know how to hit on me," she interrupts.

"Fair enough," I interject my thoughts back into words, "At least you seem to know what you're doing. And in a mean way, you're nice. I didn't come to see Quay. I came to get away from my own shit, but now I'm here and on my first night some girl goes to the hospital and I'm suddenly around people who are talking about... talking about . . . killing someone, that's what they're plotting about?"

She looks unsure of herself. Her eyes swing between kindness and cruelty. Like behind their fierceness is some plea begging to be seen behind the words. She holds up a hand, "Tell you what I am going to do. Usually I only do this for people I know. I am going to give you a 10% discount on that bottle of wine. Which means it's only 470Q."

I toss the money on the table. She bags up the wine with a patronizing smile, hands me the sealed paper bag, and waves me out the door with an intense smile.

CHAPTER FOURTEEN

The last three days, my schedule has settled into a sort of routine. I keep busy. Or at least, I feel like I'm keeping busy. I'm outside my house and off my couch, and life is no longer some future plan, it's all happening around me. During the mornings, I go to Quay's school to volunteer. We greet each other and talk about stupid, irrelevant things having nothing to do with the imminent, relevant stuff both of us are thinking about when we talk. Sometimes I volunteer in the afternoon, but other times I just wander around Antigua and observe and meet other travelers who seem to mean it when they say it was nice to meet me.

I thought volunteering in the school would have involved interacting with kids. Instead they have armed me with a broom and a rag. I sweep floors and wash windows. They hand me a hose and I water plants. I help Pablo with the upkeep. It still feels significant. It's something. The children inside the school can look out and see the beauty I helped make.

Pablo is pleasant company to work with. He keeps a social silence as he directs me to complete various tasks. Sometimes we trade words from our native languages back and forth. He is a much faster learner than I. He's very interested to learn American slang.

"What is up in the woods?"

"No, it's 'what is up in the hood?'"

Most of the slang I teach him nobody ever uses, slang I have learned from listening to rap. But I also teach him useful proverbs for an English-speaking life in our modern world.

"Bros before hoes." It means that if a girl gets in the way of a friendship, choose the friendship over the girl."

"But what about the girl loves the boy?" Pablo stops his broom mid-sweep, "I mean to say, what if the man love the girl so much. Will not the friend want the love to be?"

"It's like, if both friends are in love with the girl, better to lose the girl than the friendship."

"No, is better for one to find happiness," his softness yields to certainty, "than for both not to find the love."

And maybe he's right. Surely this saying is bullshit. But I uphold it, "No, it's better for the friendship to live on and for both friends to never find love."

"This is strange to me."

"Don't read too much into it. I think it mostly applies to one-night stands."

"One-night stands?"

"Love that only lasts one night."

I raise my eyebrows and Pablo looks again to the sky, from where he seems to intuit his deepest certainties. "But love only starts, then never ends," he says. Maybe he's seen too many American chick flicks.

"People get divorced all the time," I say wishing I was on his side of the argument.

Pablo nods his head. He knows this to be true but seems more comfortable dancing in the realm of ideals. He looks like he is about to say something but instead just shuffles his broom across the school's stone path. Finally he looks up at me, "You have been loved?"

I start, "You mean to ask me if I have been in love?"

"Sí" he nods.

I stop sweeping and the light inside my head shines into a void, searching through the ashes of feelings that have burned out. There were certain girls, at certain times I thought of those confusing but simple four letters. There was Cathy. If those feelings at those times were anything, it doesn't really matter now. I know the mechanics of what happened and that's enough. Now the cases are too cold to worry about what emotion was fueling the fire.

"I don't know," I tell Pablo sweeping my dust pile into a diamond.

"Then no? Because you would know if you were in love."

"Have you been in love?"

"Yes."

For a while there is only silence between us. I break it by asking a question that I've avoided the past few days. "Pablo," he stops sweeping as if he knows what's coming, "You know about the things people are saying? Do you know what Quay is planning to do?"

"Yes." He turns away and continues to sweep, "I give him the idea. I tell him we must do this. Then he talk to everyone, so we make a plan."

I don't believe what I'm hearing. Not Pablo, with his quiet ways and easy smile. He's not involved with this. He did not plant this idea. He is not complicit.

"Pablo, you're talking about killing someone? K-illing. Taking someone who is alive and taking that life away from them. How could you be part of something like that?"

He pauses and waits a long time before answering. "For me it is the only right thing to do. Shannon was almost killed because of the man. A bad, evil man does these things. We must do this to protect other people who he will hurt in the future."

"You're not the law Pablo, you don't get to decide who lives and who dies."

"You don't understand."

"It's not complicated. You are planning to kill someone and you don't have the right to decide that."

"Who does?" he asks, almost condescendingly. "In your country you have things that work. Bad men go to jail. Bad men go to die, yes? Here they are free. Free, free, free. Here they win and the good lose and lose and lose. My father, he lose. My mother, she lose. My brother, he lose. And they say the war is over? But it only ended on paper. The war is still here. The people are still poor and no one helps us and for me, this is the right thing to do." His voice has steadily grown in volume and confidence and somehow, even fluency.

Seeing that I have nothing more to say he adds, "For you, doing the right thing is to do nothing. But for us here, for me, doing the right thing is to do something. Let us both do the right thing, or he will just hurt more people. I will let you do what is right for you with no judging. But please let me do what is right for me with no judging. I want to still be your friend."

And ultimately, who am I to come here and tell people how to be? What is a court system but a bunch of people who got together and decided what the rules were and laid out the consequences for breaking them? What is the law but people deciding that some people have failed so much that they don't deserve their life or freedom? But the deepest parts within me that I can touch know this is not a solution, it's another problem—is feeding vicious cycles of injustice that repeat themselves again and again and again.

I sneeze the dust being kicked up from my broom and look around at the kids standing in line for lunch. It's amazing how orderly they are, how youthful wildness can be tamped down enough for a disciplined line to form. "Pablo," I say as warmly as I can, "I won't judge you. Just do me a favor; don't be so sure of yourself. If I'm learning anything here, it's that I'm wrong about a lot of things. Be open to being wrong."

He nods and holds tight to his broom but I see in his eyes that he has already chosen his path. When the afternoon ends, I return my cleaning supplies to the dilapidated tool shed where they live. Pablo walks up to me as I'm departing. "People do not listen to me. They listen to Quay. I will not do this alone. If Quay decides that no, maybe everyone decides that no."

His eyes burn. Without compromising what he believes is right, he's given me a way to stop him, "Why would you tell me that?"

"Because," he says with an innocent grin, "you are my friend, and because maybe I am wrong."

CHAPTER FIFTEEN

Quay is like vinegar confined in a small container with baking soda. He doesn't walk—he marches—his shoes keeping rhythm on the pavement. On the way to the bar, he gestures to the panorama, "All this, Liam, is ours!"

The street is mostly empty. He has laid claim to a few beggars, a drunk passed out in a urine-stained corner, some garbage, a crumbling ruin. He stops and moonwalks before catching up to me, doing a combination of walking and the river dance. Darkness is inhaling the light. It seems later than it is as the color fades to gray. It's still early though, 5:30 p.m., and I've invited Quay to come with me straight from his work to the same bar he took me to the first night, El Loco Tigre Mono.

"We need to have a do-over there," I told him, thinking how he'd do anything to do that night over. Alcohol is what we need. Alcohol is the only thing that will open him up, the only thing that might put him in a state where I can smash his conviction before he does something he can never take back.

"I always come to this bar when I go out," says Quay, slumping onto a stool. "They have okay pasta here. Stay away from the fish though, unless you want the Mayans' revenge."

"Mayans' revenge?"

"Explosive diarrhea that makes you feel like you're dying."

"Roger that."

"It's also called rocket diarrhea... because it comes out like a rocket."

"Yeah, I understood the adjective. I'll avoid the fish."

"There are many names for diarrhea here: hurtful muffins, call of the wild, the irrefutable beckoning of the porcelain throne, the untamed dragon of burning—"

"—I get it. No fish."

The bar is lit with a dozen faces. A familiarity from the first night lingers. The faces are new, but a bar is only ever different degrees of itself—an Irish laugh here, a table of Australian mates cheering for some reason, clinking glasses, music just loud enough to make conversations challenging—it's early, but it's Friday and already everyone is speaking that nocturnal language native to bars.

Sara comes up to our table to take our drink order. She gives Quay and me the customary kiss on the cheek. When it's my turn I manage to make it awkward. I offer my left cheek when I should have offered my right. There's a pause, a recalculation and after the cheek kiss is correctly performed she pulls back and directs her eyes away from me. The truth is this greeting gesture of a kiss on the cheek conducted between males and females at the time of hello is not a kiss at all. It's a cheek touching while using the lips to make the sound of a kiss and a lot can go wrong.

Quay orders us Cuba libres, "Heavy on the freedom for mine." he says

Sara gives me a sober smile, her eyes laughing at me, she glances over at Quay and a silent understanding passes between them.

"For the liberation of Cuba!" Quay raises the glass Sara delivers to his quick hand.

I raise my glass to meet his, "Cheers man."

"CUBA!" he shouts so loud he quiets our corner of the bar as patrons pause to assess.

"Why are you so hung up on the Cuba thing?" I ask after we drink.

"That's what these drinks are for. Every dollar from every Cuba Libre sold goes to the freedom of Cuba." He has already downed his drink and I see him and I remember Quay. This is the Quay I knew from school. Quay the uncompromising, Quay who's water bottle carried vodka, always teetering on the edge with the powers that were in those days.

He orders another round and glances at my half-full glass, "Liam, when's the last time you've been with a woman?"

Maybe he was glancing at my half-empty glass. I finish the rest in one long slow draw. I take a moment to let the brain freeze pass. "Quay, I don't know what the hell you're doing down here. Really, I haven't wrapped my brain around it, but I know it's why I'm here, and I know I want to be here, and I sort of forgot what that felt like, you know?"

Quay ignores me and waves two fingers to Sara.

"I made a promise to myself when I dropped out," he sips from his glass, "never to use my present as a means to my future. Never to do something I didn't want to do as a means to something I wanted to do. So college couldn't happen and I stayed true to that."

Sara sets the drinks on our table. Then I see my life through his eyes. I wonder what he thinks about my life. Since the...accidents...the tragedies...the stuff I don't talk about. But the stuff you don't talk about takes up so much more space than the stuff you do. It's always here, always behind every corner of conversation. But it's not like this with Quay. I get the impression he genuinely doesn't give a shit, and that's a safe space I can rest in. He is a huge pain in the ass and an unwavering asshole, but his self-absorption is a virtue to me. It keeps him from caring about the things that everyone wants to talk to me about, and I just want to be left alone.

He's still going on. "So many people put off their happiness to a later date, but they don't realize that you can't do that. They let employers waste their time doing crap. They con themselves into thinking they're happy."

I tell him I agree, but maybe I don't. Maybe those other people are the happy ones. Maybe Quay is the one playing the con game and saying all this to convince himself. I tune back into the conversation only when I realize that he's asked me a question. "What would you do if someone broke into your house and stole your TV?"

"I would punch him in the face," I tell him, swigging until the ice cubes calf in my glass, "Then I would drop kick him."

"Would you call the police and want him arrested?"

"Sure."

Quay slams his glass down, "You would call the police yeah?!"

I slam my glass down too, "I would call the police dammit!"

"And they would come?" Quay nods up and down and suddenly I understand what's being discussed within this guise when he says. "Well here, doesn't matter, you can call the police and be damn sure they are not coming. Justice here doesn't begin with a call to the cops, Liam."

We pause for a second and look at two incoming girls. I turn back to Quay, "How big's the TV? Is it plasma screen?"

No, I think. This might not be Quay. Not yet. He's still trying out this personality, this iteration of himself. The glue hasn't yet taken hold. That's what this conversation is about. He's reinforcing that this is in fact who he is. Maybe that's what we all have to be worried about, we may really be someone else. Quay goes to the bathroom and I imagine a way to subtly broach the reason I came out with him.

He comes back and all I manage is the blunted edge, "How's the murder plot shaping up?"

But he comes back with one better, "That you're calling it that shows that you don't understand what's happening and why. I'm sorry that this had to happen now, I know it's very inconvenient for your vacation."

I crunch what remains of my rum and Coke's ice, "Do you know the difference between a believer and a non-believer, Quay?"

He looks away, "Do tell."

He's not open to listening. He just wants to talk. Everyone just wants to talk and no one wants to listen. I swirl the dead lime in my glass, "After a non-believer has a psychotic episode, he gets help. A believer has a hallucination and thinks it's heaven-sent and uses that psychosis to convince ten non-believers to believe in his imaginary friend."

"What's your point?"

"Quay, God as presented by the major religions is a narcissistic bastard. He's a bastard for putting all kinds of great things in the world and not allowing us to have them and then trying to make us love him even while he won't even show himself definitively. So know that I'm not throwing you some thou-shalt-not-do-this edict—ultimately you're going to do what you do—but an eye for an eye, or karma, or whatever it is that governs this thing called the universe—cause and effect seem as real to me as anything I have known. It's not just about what you are planning to do, but what comes from it."

He turns and looks at me straight in the eye, "Do you blame yourself in some way?"

And my reaction is one of mistaken identity. I want to ask him to clarify exactly what he means to make sure he is not talking about what I know he is. So I say, "We're having a good time, yeah? Let's just drink and talk about anything but religion."

79

I feel my frustration and fear rise, but I am a coward, so I smile them into oblivion. This has not gone as planned. But there's enough alcohol for a fresh start and both of us just need more of that.

"Do you know what we need?" I ask Quay.

"What?"

"Shots."

After Sara drops off our second round of shots, we talk about sports. About how neither of us follows them, and how sometimes guys who are perpetually baseball-capped hold this against us. The rift between us contracts and breaks. After another round we bask in a light buzz. For now, we can just be two old friends enjoying each other's company without needing to talk about anything worthwhile. Quay slams his glass down on the table and must already be drunk, "You see that pair of Swedish chicks over there?"

"Don't point at them. How do you know they are Swedish?"

"Dude, look at 'em."

I see two blonde girls that could be easily from anywhere in the US. They are not the sort of women who should be approached for any reason. They are too beautiful, demanding commensurate perfection or lavish wealth. Whoever these girls are, they have hidden themselves behind bronzed skin and sun-blessed hair that should terrify us all. Hiding behind light blue eyes are two humans who give me a valid reason to hate my own genetic makeup. I am not ugly, but these women are the children of deities. They are not from this world. Earthlings should be allowed no access to them. Shame on these goddesses who taint all of the others in the bar.

But it's easy to forgive them on behalf of their cleavage. Cleavage and smiles. Smiles and teeth that make smiling worthwhile. Laser-cut white teeth and cleavage that turns ordinary men into poets. The sort of cleavage that gives you a glimpse of eternity. Cleavage worth writing home about. Cleavage that gives you just enough to imagine what you'd do if you had access to what was behind that magical curtain. This is the cleavage that drives men to gyms, hoping that if they can sculpt their body into something more, this cleavage will open up to them.

Quay follows my gaze, "See, definitely Swedish."

"Do not talk to them."

"Why?"

"They are out of our league."

"League?" he stands and backs up from word, "What the hell is that? They're not like American girls. They don't know that they're beautiful, because that's just how all women look in Sweden. There's the people that go for it, Liam, and the little piggies who cry wee wee wee all the way home. There's no league." He pounds his fists on his chest as an expression of his leaguelessness.

I scan the room and see two homely girls tucked away in a dark corner. "Look at those girls over there, let's talk to them instead."

"Coward"

"Realist."

"Let's send them a drink."

"Order me at least three shots of Tequila before you do."

"Have you always been like this? I don't remember you being like this. You weren't like this in high school. Bring that Liam back. You're in Guatemala, nothing matters."

He's right. I've spent this whole trip telling myself that same thing, begging my mind to shut up for once in its life. I always plan on being someone other than I am, but when the future comes, here I am, still trapped in me.

Quay waves the bartender over in a way that would have made me want to cut him when I was a bartender, but Sara skips over to him. He asks her to send the two girls a round of waters from us.

"You're sending waters?" Seated behind us are two cleavage-goddesses, demanding worship, rejecting all offerings, condemning to terrible deaths any slimy morons who think themselves worthy of speaking to them. Chinese water torture—death by Alice Cooper. Or perhaps worse—life with Alice Cooper.

"Yeah, water. I am an NGO volunteer. I can't even pay for these drinks." He points to our empty glasses. "I can't invest anything on them, you see?" I brace myself for an explanation that will not make sense to anyone sober, "their beauty means that guys probably buy them drinks all the time…"

Quay is still talking, but I allow whatever he is saying to drown in the drone of the bar and I turn to Sara sans H. "Two shots of tequila please." She glides giddily to pour the shots and her glee must be due to some illegal substance. She sighs, setting one in front of me and one in front of Quay and I grab both, quickly absorbing the first into my blood, knowing that a right mind would never be privy to the logic that Quay is spewing at me. There is an honesty in vile shots of gross tequila. It's not about enjoying anything. There is no pretense. It's horrible. It makes you hate your life for a second. It's about getting smashed as quickly as possible. The world needs more honesty like tequila.

Quay is still talking. "...but if we send them waters, we set ourselves apart... "

I take my second shot. "Thuuuaaaaa!" Tequila is devil water. I live through it.

Quay's rant tapers off with the same meaninglessness that it began with, "...so don't worry."

I envy his blind stupidity, wonder if that is another name for confidence, and plan to drink myself to this level. I face the bar, watching through the mirror behind the many bottles as our obviously stoned bartender sets down the two glasses of water and points to us. I wait for their perfect smiles to drop in disgust as our gift is rejected. I always seem to be stuck with friends with shameless people. I can see from the mirror behind the bottles shelved at the bar that one of the girls has taken a drink of her water. Quay orders us each a shot of devil water, which tastes like frustration. I gag. My disgusted tongue is determined to make me nauseous.

"Sheeza, no more tequila."

I nearly fall down. I need to slow down. There is plenty of night left that those bottles behind the bar will steal away if I let them.

The Swedish girls are waving at someone. They are waving at us. They want us to come over to them. I hate Quay. We approach their table. Rather, Quay approaches the table and due to some sort of awkward magnetism, I follow behind.

"Hola ladies!"

"Hi boys! How did you guys know that we wanted waters?"

"Because you looked so hot!" Quay blurts out with the enthusiasm of a drunken ape swinging feces maracas. My face flushes because I feel the embarrassment he should. But you should never use the word should, and the girls are laughing. Apparently, Quay is hilarious and he makes their tanned breasts bounce rhythmically with their joviality.

"It may taste a little funny," says Quay, "But that's just from the poison my friend Liam put in it!"

Both girls laugh at this and this is shocking. If I had made a poison joke it just would not have gone over, period. It's time for the ubiquitous name exchange. Gabriella is wearing a blue tank top that fits her perfectly. She is sitting to the right of Karina. Karina is wearing a gold sparkly tank top with a white dress shirt unbuttoned over the top of it to show her bust to the world. The world is thankful. They are indeed from Sweden, and this causes me to love Quay, but to hate him too. Quay is wild. Out of control, more like an animal pretending to be human. A smashed ape with a glass of rum in one hand and a fire stick in the other. Yet the girls are amused at everything he utters and everything I have learned about the world, about women, and life in general over the last twenty-six years is incorrect. I take a breath. The world isn't crashing down around me. The girls are nice. Kind. Smiling. Even at me.

I wish for things to say. But all I am doing is ironically repeating things that Quay says, so that I can personalize some of the laughter bouncing across the table. I want to let go of everything—myself, my indignation at Quay's ludicrousness, my past and learn to just be here on earth with the rest of the humans. Like Quay. It is time to elect other aspects of myself. Time to meld myself into this moment and burn away my insecurities that more and more have no place inside me. I justify myself to myself because, had things been different, I would be someone else. But how can I explain that to strangers? I deserve a light touch and acceptance, and boundless love, but how to explain this to everyone I meet?

"Heyo!" A tall, tan man embraces Gabriella from behind.

"Timmy!" Gabriella exclaims, wild with excitement.

Quay raises his glass to Timmy's bottle while chanting, "Timmy-timmy-timmy-timmy-timmy!" I give the what's up nod and he nods back. He is my homie now and he has come to steal the woman who is her own.

Gabriella is riotous, she grabs Timmy and demands, "Where is Tommy?"

In answer Tommy appears from behind Timmy with a freshly ordered drink. Karina sighs, relieved that Timmy has not lost Tommy. I give Tommy a what's up nod, and he spreads a wing of an arm in an elaborated wind-up to high five to handshake. Now Tommy is my homie too. Tommy and Timmy pull up stools. There are six of us crowding around a table for four. Both Tommy and Timmy are Australian and tan and tall—the hearty offspring of Britain's prisoners who survived the boat ride.

An initial reaction to dislike them due to their evolutionary genetic superiority is soon eclipsed by their joviality.

"It's a good thing I didn't bring my axes to the bar!" Tommy yells, responding to something I did not hear Karina say.

"Yeah, it's a good thing," I mumble like furniture might say were it to speak.

The waitress brings me a rum and coke and I drink it quickly hoping a certain self will emerge, a self I am not sure I ever was, but one I desperately need now. Timmy raises his glass and puts his hand on my shoulder, "To our new American mates!" Six glasses crash in the center.

Then the stories begin. Stories that lead to other stories, unrelated, different, the same, melding perfectly, a melody of traveled pasts eagerly shared. Gabriella and Karina tell us about León, Nicaragua, a place they had traveled through en route to Antigua. The gist is that they met a constantly-rum-infused man from Cuba claiming to be the half brother of Fidel Castro.

León, Nicaragua? Tommy asks. Or is he Timmy, Did they stay in the Bigfoot Hostel? Yes, they did. There is some talk about this hostel, the goods, the bads, and the volcano boarding. Volcano boarding apparently is careening down a volcano at 70 k/hr on a wooden sled. They recall how they had smoked a blunt with two Israelis prior to volcano boarding.

"Israelis are crazy and always high," Gabriella says, and she smiles at me.

"In my experience that's 100% true," I say.

"Yeah and one of the Israelis broke his shoulder," Tommy adds.

Quay mentions how he had climbed Pacaya, here in Guatemala and roasted marshmallows in the lava, recommending that everyone do the same. He nods at me telling me that we will go there. Karina has climbed a volcano in Panama, Barú, and nearly froze to death at the top, Tommy almost froze to death in the ocean off the coast of Chile, "My guide book was right, bloody rotten swimming there!"

A dog in Chile bit Timmy on his legs, ass, and elbow and he worried he had rabies. Be he decided to roll the dice and not get the rabies vaccination when he found it involved multiple shots through the belly button. Gabriella points out that we probably would not notice even if Timmy were to become rabid and to that Timmy growls and gyrates while biting the air.

Another round is ordered, the Australians insist on paying for this one. Bartender Sara looks destroyed, like she's sleep sprinting.

Four little dogs used to bark all night until one day Quay saw that all four had been beheaded with a machete. Karina makes a puppy face and seems torn about this tidbit until Timmy starts barking and Tommy pretends to behead him with a fork.

Empty glasses are replaced. For the moment, I forget who I am because I simply am somewhere I belong. The Australian's joviality is liberally handed out to all, indiscriminate and without hesitation. I take as much as my hands can hold, trying to absorb them completely, willing to vacate myself to make room for an upgrade. I add too little to the conversation, but somewhere in my background, I can feel a younger me looking out, feeling proud at merely being present. My eyes from a month ago look out from the couch where he spent all day and he says, yeah, this is better than that, thank you. He peers into an empty bottle of Jack and the colors of the past and present bleed together creating a new color.

Karina complains about the prices in Sweden, and Quay nods saying that it was $30 for a whiskey coke.

Has Quay been to Sweden?

My eyes tip-toe to Gabriella and she smiles back and this glimpse is great and scary and I wonder what I will do, if anything, and where it would lead me, if anywhere. I haven't been with a girl in so long and who knows if I remember all the steps to that ageless dance. Slow scans of the room allow my eyes to accidentally fall on the bright cleavage between her light blue tank top, royally tanned, vision trap. When telling a story, she is loud and confident, but when listening, seems to be communicating only with me, gauging my reaction to the punch lines, laughing when I laugh.

Quay and her go to the bathroom at the same time and when Quay returns he takes her seat and she comes back and sits next to me. Gabriella laughs and says on her way back from the bathroom someone tried to sell her cocaine and in unison both of the Australians sing, "Bloody Bogotá!"

Both shake their heads in disbelief of the memory they are about to summon, shocked that the world could allow such an ongoing.

"Oh man, last Chrissie it was." Tommy keeps shaking his head, and Quay and I exchange glances.

"Talk about a guster, thought we was gonna be locked up."

"He was bits from being thrown in the bloody can!"

These guys have flow. They have it.

"We were staying in a hostel in Bogotá with this bloody wanker last Chrissie yeah?—and he comes strolling over to us like, 'mates, do you realize it's Christmas?' Says he's from Melbourne, something about his accent though, seemed a bit Irish."

"Convinces us that we should get some blow." They are a team, one person occupying two bodies.

"Says, 'Mates, it is bloody Christmas and we're bored shitless sitting in a bloody hostel. What we need is some sniff sniff.'"

"Now, of course, Tommy and I have accidentally smelled some white powder too hard once or twice, but it's still time for brekkie and all I want are some eggs and bacon."

Tommy continues the story so Timmy can take a swig of his Cuba. "Now, he was a good fellow Alex from what we knew, a bit of a dag, the night before all three of us were off our face in the hostel, nowhere else was open because everyone was off on holiday, and we was the only ones staying, all I'm thinking about is eggs or pancakes, but Alex really wants to get some blow."

"I hear the stuff's addictive," I say to laughter.

Tommy continues, "Tells us about, how for him, it's a Christmas tradition."

"Every Christmas, Alex has gotten himself off his rocker with a big bag of blow."

"Now, Timmy and I are not people who break traditions."

"So, we say we'll give it a whirl, 'Alex, but where we gonna get blow on Christmas?' we ask him."

"Tells us he knows this guy who's told him where to go. Tells us it's gonna be fifty US dollars each, and we say, 'Fifty US dollars for blow?'"

"Remember this here is Colombia, where coke costs as much as sand does in Saudi Arabia."

The Swedish girls think this depiction is exceptionally funny, and while they laugh Tommy and Timmy down their drinks and catch the red-eyed Sara as she passes our table. I look around and notice that the table behind us seems to be intently listening to the story. Quay notices me noticing the table and mumbles "Germans," indicating with a nod the table behind me.

"So—", The Australians lose their place. After a pause Tommy triumphantly yells, "Fifty American dollars!" and Timmy continues.

"Yeah! Fifty bloody American dollars for blow. But Alex says that it's the best, pure, and enough to last us the whole day. He's got us convinced that Christmas would be ruined without blow, so we get our fifty dollars, and I'm starting to feel like this idea is a good idea, that we buy some coke and have us a Christmas rage."

"After all, we were just gonna sit around the hostel, callin' our oldies to say sorry for being away for another Chrissie."

"So, we give Alex the money and he insists that we go with him to buy the stuff."

"There is no traffic and we take a cabbie to this nasty part of town."

"Right away I think—"

"This guy was about to wet his shorts—"

"Oh, and you weren't scared at all?"

They laugh and simultaneously take a large swig of their drinks. Everyone at our table lifts their glasses too, the Australians controlling the pace of our consumption with their story.

"I reckon we was both wanting our mums when we gets to where we was going."

"So we walk into this dark alley a couple of kilometers from the hostel—it's a bad neighborhood, we're ready to get shot, and there is just this door, Alex says this is the place, and I say, 'I'm not going in there,' then I realize that it's much better than staying out in this dodgy alley."

"It wasn't completely abandoned, there was this guy lookin' real dodgy, like he wants to jump us."

"So we ring the bell, and no one comes, at this point we're both ready to go back, to get the bloody hell out. But our hero Alex says to wait and that someone is coming and sure enough someone comes and he gives us a real good lookin' down."

"Says, 'come in' like a real gangster."

"And he's a big, big dude."

"So this place has shit all over the wall, and franger wrappers just lying about, wadded toilet paper on a floor that hasn't been swept since the Queen was in charge. He takes us down this long hall with a bunch of closed doors, and we are both thinking 'we are going to die.'"

"And like, the only sound is coming from the floor above us where we hear someone screaming."

"And we can't tell if it's in ecstasy or pain."

"Oh, it was someone shagging for sure."

"We were both about to piss our shorts."

The pair takes another pause to allow us to sink into the gravity of the story. My eyes make and break contact with Gabriella's. Somewhere behind these, conducting that beautiful body, is someone.

The Australians relight their tale, "I don't know how walls could ever get so filthy. It looked
like an elephant had been shitting on the walls."

It's Tommy's turn to talk and Timmy's to drink, "So we wait at the end of the hall, all the while someone is being shagged or killed or something on the floor above us.

"And Alex hasn't said diddly to us, he's just looking around like waiting for the bus."

"The guy comes back with a small ziplock bag of white powder and says $100."

"And Alex getting angry at the giant guy!"

88

"And so I'm like to hell with this," says Timmy, "And I hand him one hundred fucking USDs and Alex takes the bag and we get out of there as fast as we can without making it seem like we were fleeing."

Tommy takes over, "We don't walk two blocks when here come the police. They ask to search us and of course, it's not okay that they find blow on Alex. And what does this guy do? He tells the police that it's ours and not his! Well the police are ready to lock all three of us up and I'm imagining what it looks like inside a Colombian jail, and what kind of cellmates to expect, when Tommy, who speaks a bit of Spanish starts trying to bribe them, and luckily all the police are corrupt and they bite, but they want at least five-hundred US dollars, which is much better than getting locked up, so we go to a cash machine,"

"But the most I can take out is three-hundred American dollars in one day and I say, look man, this is all I got, and the police take it and tell us to get in the car."

"And I'm thinking it's all over, that we are going off to jail and goodbye."

"All the while Alex is looking like a bloody idiot, not saying anything, even though he's the one who got us into this mess, he's the dude who had blow on him, he's the dude that hasn't spent a dollar on this ordeal.

"Well, then the police turns and asks us in English, 'Where are you staying?'"

"We tell him and sure enough, he takes us back to the hostel, tells us merry Christmas, and drives away."

We start to show our incredulity at the occurrence when Tommy motions with his hands that there's still more, "Well then, we get back and are just happy to be back and I decide to eat so much breakfast and then get drunk and I'm in the hammock, and guess who's head appears and says, 'I know of another place where we can get some blow."

"That guy." Tommy takes a drink and looks off into the distance, "absolute legend of a mess of a failed human."

"Cheers to fucking Alex," says Timmy.

We clink glasses in honor of the dishonorable Alex and I wonder what has become of him. Is he still in Colombia? Has he become a guerilla warfare fighter? Was he killed by a drug dealer? By a drug? Has he opened a comic and ceramics shop?

Most likely, he has quietly slipped away in the world I'm just learning exists, an international undertow where people easily drift and drown.

Timmy finishes his drink smiling and he has every reason to be smiling. It is pure and true and I am elated by his deserved delight. Tommy slaps him on the back and lights a cigarette and leans out the iron caged windowsill, breathing in the smoke like supple redemption. The soft grayness he exhales twists shapelessly into the night and a light haze surrounds us all. Gabriella moves closer to me until our legs are touching. She's done it on purpose, wants our legs to touch, and she is not just a beautiful girl in a bar, she seems a real possibility for tonight, for forever, maybe there is no difference. This is how people meet, how lives together begin. We are each others' for at least right now, making the most of chance before leaving, traveling north or south, direction irrelevant. And I will be staying here and then depart to the rest of my life, this table has its limitations, this life its boundaries, this bar a closing time.

But for now, Timmy smiles beyond the moment, encapsulating it fully, explaining every fleeting thing. They all have that resolve—travelers seeing only possibilities in the distances that separate our differences, absorbing people and places like light, treading in and out of each others' lives, letting go of the transient things I hold onto so tightly.

The night has been kind. As the lights turn on Sara and the other bartenders herd us to the exit, I sight that passing understanding that can be seen only in soft glimpses, as unexplainable as it is genuine and true and divine and fleeting. As we walk out to leave, I catch a wayward glimpse of Stella slipping into the bar, hurrying to the back room where she disappears behind a door. Her eyes intercept mine just as the door closes. Sara looks dreamily to the door that she's entered and sighs.

"Out! *Afuera*! Out!" The busboy is yelling."Out! Everyone!"

I walk to the door with everything intact. It's been a good night.

"You wanna see something awesome?" Quay asks us in the streetlight.

"Obviously," I answer.

"Arrrr!!!" Quay starts howling like a dog.

"That was not awesome."

"Just wait."

He howls again, louder this time.

A dog somewhere in the night starts howling. Another dog answers. Then another is howling. Soon there are hundreds of dogs howling in the street, filling the night with the sound of desperate dogs.

"Okay, that was awesome," I tell him.

Innocently and confidently, Gabriella catches me in the night air, taking my hand and pulling me into her smile. Beneath a clean, cold midnight, her lips are perfect and they implant their thirst in mine. We kiss in the street amid the uproar of howling dogs and then she pulls away from me and asks, "Do you want to show me where you're staying?"

She smiles at me meekly and we share the same conspiracy. Timmy and Tommy give me a grin. Their closed fists pound against mine and they wobble and tell me that they'll see me around, mate. Quay winks, says nothing to me, and wobbles over to Katrina. Gabriella and I are wobbling in a night that has become just ours, left alone to wobble and kiss on a dark street, dimly lit with nighttime possibility that seals into walking the path to my dorm room bunk bed.

"Do you want to show me where you are staying?" she asks me in a smiling, European accent. And I either don't remember I'm staying in a bunk bed in a room shared with others or I don't care, because I begin to lead the way. Alcohol and hormones are wonderful things to behold together. And this a woman from Sweden, knowing me for less than six hours, gorgeous like scalding water, allows me into that secret they guard and we reach for from the twisting helix in our blood.

She is there, somewhere behind her blue eyes. I turn to kiss her and Baboom-chicaoosh! To the left and to the right and up and down, a tuc-tuc motorized rickshaw I don't really remember boarding lurches through Antigua's uneven cobblestone streets toward my hostel. Baboom-chica! The driver is a maniac, and he operates his 50cc craft like a warplane. Gabriella grabs my shoulder to stabilize herself against such belligerent glee. We endeavor to touch each other's lips as the tuc-tuc hurls our inebriated bodies about the cab. Sex seems inevitable.

Gabriella is under my arm and we wobble into the entrance of my hostel. A new front desk lady looks horrified at the escapade of our entrance but we fall past her and she shudders away into a computer screen. It's nice to be close to someone, to have someone to hug and hold. You don't need to know last names because that adds nothing to what this is. This is a night to build or demolish, and so often creation and destruction are achieved with the very same tools. And thusly Gabriella and I stumble through the hostel's midnight halls. Gringos, up to their antics, that's all. Most of the lights have been turned off giving the hostel a daunting consciousness. We kiss closer and closer to my dorm room, and there seems to be more than just the two of us. I don't mean the others in my room whom we are about to wake. I mean there are a thousand facets of faces looking out of my eyes. There is the three-year-old and he is happy, but startled at how adult the view has been this past decade. He doesn't understand this at all. But there is the junior high kid, sad and insecure and he promised himself that all that would fade away by now. He swore to be done with it at awkward dances. He declared with a cracking voice, but he must see, it's all still here in his future. There is the high school kid, who stubbornly believes that his world could be changed if only he owned a vehicle. I see my eighteen-year-old self as he appears to me now, eight years later, eight years gone.

Gabriella is laughing in my bottom bunk because I am endeavoring to use my top sheets as curtains so we can have a private little chateau, but to do so I have to poke around the top bunk, waking up its sovereign, who responds to the situation with incoherent mumblings and heavy sighs which only further fuels the hilarity Gabriella feels within, fueling more laughter, waking up the other tenant of the dorm, a Canadian who is not very nice.

"This is *not* happening," he raises his voice without raising his head.

I throw the curtain I have created and place my index finger perpendicular to my lips.

"Wait," she says. She takes the bottom sheet off the bed and firms it, dusting it off. She's a genius. Our dwelling reminds me of those forts everyone made as kids. Sheets draped over tables and desks, intimate places of unmitigated imagination.

The sensation of her back shoots through arm to brain, and I feel what should be called innocence. No one wants to harm anyone here. We want to hold and touch and belong to each other, but quietly, so we don't disturb the others. While peace has not been made, a ceasefire seems to have been agreed upon. Through the concealing curtain draping over my bed, Gabriella is suddenly intimately in my life. On my bed, Gabriella lies. She allows me to put a hand on her thigh. She puts her hand atop mine to show her approval of hand-on-thigh. She puts her lips to my lips once more, to show her approval of my lips. She approves of my neck. And my ears. And my forehead. And most of my face. Small kisses course across my body. And then she begins to giggle against — and, finding her own giggling hilarious, she begins to laugh, fully beyond her control.

The occupant of the bunk above hits the wall, prompting the Canadian in the bunk across the room to yell, "It's a fucking dorm room so shut the fuck up!"

With the subtle determination of a man walking on coals, Gabriella manages to bring her laughter down to the level of quiet little giggles, prompting only a few huffs from the bed above. I want to point out to the Canadian man that his yelling was far louder than any noise we've produced, but I realize it's not such a good time for such things.

So instead I reach a hand underneath Gabriella's shirt and make myself into the big spoon, a few quiet kisses on her neck the she approves of by purring like a cross between a cat and a song-bird might purr. She places her hand over my hand. Gently. She takes it as one would hold the hand of a scared child. And like that we fall asleep, oblivious of any chance of tomorrow.

Part III
CHAPTER SIXTEEN

In ancient times, the Mayans of Guatemala searched for a more accurate description of observed reality. They thought that flowers and songs were the highest things on earth that could penetrate truth. The core of their existence was *panche be*, the search for the root of truth. I know this because the only thing I can do is read about them while failing to hold down solid foods. I didn't order the fish, but the Mayan's revenge has found me.

My bowels erupt with the force of vengeance. Cramps that I would gladly trade for death sing my song of pain. These cannot get worse. I want to be free from this body. I want to die. Without someone being born, this level of abdominal pain is not okay. How did the human body evolve to take so much pain? Invisible things torture me from the inside. For the last three days, my world has shrunk to the size of my bunk and the adjacent bathroom.

Bunk then bathroom, bathroom then bunk, back and forth in a ceaseless cycle. There is a bunk and there is a bathroom, and there is rushing from this bunk to the bathroom with the sort of urgency that saves you from doom. This is my world now. The only exercise I get is when I hold onto my stomach and sprint. I never reach the toilet with more than a few seconds to spare. A handful of times don't make it in time and am forced to throw out three of my five pairs of underwear. The Mayans are kicking my body's ass. What wouldn't I do for some Vaseline? Today I am nothing but a conduit for food and water seeking the promised, porcelain land.

I force myself into my book, to escape the painful reality of today. The hostel book exchange had romance novels and a few books on the Mayans. Not feeling exceptionally romantic, I've opted for the books on the Mayans to distract myself from the unbearable pain.

The two guys in my dorm room have since moved on since the night of the giggles, and the two new people seem alarmed by my existence. One Swedish-looking girl glares at me whenever she enters.

"Do you need anything?" A German in an inside-out yellow T-shirt wearing aviator sunglasses indoors asked me on day one of mien kampf. He laughed uncomfortably when I told him he could hold my hand the next time I used the little boy's room.

Day three of hell-on-earth-intestinal-tract: Running low on wearable clothes. Must find a cure for all diseases.

Quay enters my room just as the sound of a distant drums begins to build outside. I am holding my stomach and lamenting my existence. He uses his sleeve to clear a chair littered with used tissues and hesitates before sitting down.

Oh no…

Phew, just flatulence.

"Hey, I brought you some drugs."

"Brawwwwwww, thanks."

"…"

"What's that?" Tubas outside have joined the drums.

"Cipro, and some de-worming stuff. If it's bacterial the Cipro should kick it. If it's worms, well, the de-worming stuff should take care of it."

"Don't you need a prescription for that?" Trombones have come in behind trumpets, which are climbing to higher notes.

Quay laughs, "You're south of the border hombre. You're your own doctor here. As long as you can pronounce the name of the medicine, they'll sell it to you."

"Good to know."

"This stuff should start to kick in within twenty-four hours. Unfortunately the de-worming stuff is probably going to make you nauseous."

"More nauseous?"

"Worms don't go without a fight. Maybe take the Cypro first and if that doesn't kill whatever's living inside of you, then take the worm stuff. Unless you caught H. Pylori which is transmissible from kissing." Quay can't help but smirk.

"Joy," I say, holding my stomach like my hands could heal.

"Welcome to my country," Quay says in a Latin accent and beams like a third-grader who's won a 4-H ribbon. The music begins to drown out our voices.

"Thanks," I say over the blaring band. This makes my tone sound nastier than I want it to.

Quay chuckles. He is kind. Today he is my friend and I am grateful. He tells me he'll come back and check on me later. God bless him. And goddamn, this is either a bout of flatulence, or I will need to do laundry. He seems about to leave, but lingers, examining uninteresting objects around the room. The walls are beginning to shake with what must be some sort of matching apocalypse on the other side. With some hesitation Quay stands up and shouts down at me over the thundering outside. "Shannon is going in for surgery tomorrow. It's to rebuild her sinuses or something like that—"

"Have you guys—"

"Not yet." I read his lips.

"What are you waiting for?"

". . . no real rush . . . want to make sure we've thought everything through."

"If you haven't done it yet, I don't think you're going to do it." I yell over the noise, swallowing two of the pills.

"I did listen to what you said. We even went police to file a report hoping they would do what they're supposed to do. But nada. They don't care. They're just kids with uniforms and guns—"

"I'm too sick to care what you do—"

Quay brings his face close to mine and shouts over the ruckus, "You've only been here a week, Liam. I would've thought the same way. But I've been here for two years and I understand things differently now. Americans . . . we take justice for granted. We expect it. To us it's something removed. Something that other people are in charge of protecting. It's not like that here. We are those other people—"

This is ridiculous. Anything he wants to say is being smothered by trumpets, and booming drums, and trombones, and snare drums, and clarinets and french horns—all playing siege music written to break down walls

"What the strange hell is going on out there?"

I miss every third word, "Palm Sunday... Procession... Start of Holy Week... Shit's gonna hit the fan this week." He walks to the other end of the room and runs his fingers across the wooden frame of my neighbor's bunk. I see something in his eyes I did not notice before, a certain sadness that's holding him. Details from the first night flash nonsensically in my thoughts. Shannon disappearing. Quay disappearing. The dog running around the bar. Both reappearing. The bloody nose.

The climax has past and the music fades away at the pace it faded in. "It was you, wasn't it?"

Quay seems struck by a blow, but says nothing. Maybe he didn't even hear me. We sit and listen to the music die. When you can just barely make out a rhythm in the distance, I turn to his back turned to me. "It was you who bought the drugs. That's what this is about. You hurt her."

He looks in the direction that the music disappeared, wishing it would return. He won't look at me.

"With that kinda guilt I can't imagine anyone could make a rational decision about anything."

"I'm meeting a friend for lunch," he says still without facing me. "I just came to see how you were. I'll stop by later and see if the drugs kicked in."

"Thanks," I say to his departing back. He's soon replaced by a girl checking in and setting her backpack on the unoccupied bunks.

"Are you okay?" she asks.

"Don't eat the food here," I tell her.

She looks confused, so I decide to confuse her more. "Did you know it was common for the Mayans to practice self-torture? Almost every major political happening required bloodletting." I indicate the book with a Mayan codex on the cover lying next to me. "Royal blood was necessary. Obviously. If I were a god, I would be pretty pissed off if they were only giving me peasant blood. The king and his wives and other members of the royal family would cut themselves open to produce a blood offering."

"I hadn't heard that," she says, hesitating to leave her bag alone with me in the room, but equally uncomfortable to stay here alone with me. I guess anything can be a sacred ritual. Mix imagination and a naïve peasant population, and my trips to the bathroom could become a prayer. I'll never know—no one will—but I doubt the Mayan kings really believed spilling their blood was accomplishing anything. Are no beliefs too absurd?

There was something spiritual in their pain. There is nothing spiritual about my agony. I don't eat. I can hardly sleep. I can only respond to nature's screaming call. Language has not produced invectives vile enough to describe any of this. I take a healthy drink of the Gatorade Quay left me and fall asleep.

When I wake up, I still feel wrecked, but fixed enough to think thoughts beyond the happenings of my body. Lying in bed with a low fever burning, I drift between different worlds until I am on top of the volcano looking at the valley and cities below. From above, I see Antigua from afar, but it seems much closer, or at least, clearer. Fire burns in bright audacious clouds above. I place my hand on my forehead and can feel a silky sweat. There are no roads. There are no birds. There is no color green. There is a man on the mountain with me and he is looking at the city, shaking his head. The city is impossible. It has been wrecked and there are bodies everywhere. But then the city opens like a flower. From up so high, I can see that the blossoming city is really more like a lake. A rainbow lake so clear that I can see valleys and colorful trees underneath.

Without turning to face me he asks, "Do you ever wonder?"

I tell him that yes, sometimes I do, and he continues to shake his head and pose questions, "Do you ever wonder what it would be like today if the West hadn't caused our bloody civil war?"

"No," I tell him, "I never wondered that."

There are Mayans in the city and they are letting their blood. But the blood does not flow far. It is peasant blood. They let out more blood, waiting for the rich red blood of kings to come. But the blood does not flow and the Mayans are as far below as the past is willing to stretch.

He shakes his head, "Do you ever wonder what it would be like if they had not crossed the Ocean? If the Mayans had been able to choose their own future?"

"No, I never wonder that."

"Do you ever wonder," and there is something broken about the man, "Do you ever wonder what Antigua would be like if those earthquakes had not destroyed her?"

"Yes," I say, "I wonder that." I nod while the man shakes his head.

We are up too high, I want to tell him. We can never cross the mountains, can never come down. I know that the mountains he gazes at cannot be crossed, but I know that he will never believe me and I don't have a mouth. Where my mouth used to be is a fresh layer of skin. The man shakes his head and looks up at the bleeding sky, the fire clouds move across the volcano. There is so much more to tell him.

There are important things I have been saving up, but when I look for them, they are gone and I have no mouth to say anything. This must be why he can only shake his head, because of the many important, forgotten things.

"Do you ever wonder," he says, "who I'd be today?" The man turns. I see his frightful face and all his questions melt to nothing more than sad speculation. These will not lead anyone anywhere. The man is my father; so I am dreaming. And I see them. I see something mammoth-like below the oceanic ice, the thoughts I don't allow myself to think. Simple alternatives, how things might have gone had they not gone as they did.

In my dream, my dead father reaches towards my face, but I open my eyes before he touches me. Above me the wood of the upper bunk holds up a mattress. My body somewhere foreign, my mind is daring to imagine things I thought it had forgotten to think.

CHAPTER SEVENTEEN

It's only after walking to the bathroom post afternoon nap that I realize I feel better. My next bowel movement shows heartening signs of solidity. I've been cooped up in this hostel room; a prisoner to my own body for too long and I need air. The woman at reception looks at me with worried eyes. I am that guy. The one who has something not right with him. The one who came back drunk with Gabriella.

"Estás mejor?"
"Sí," I manage.
"Necesitas algo?"
"Sí—"

I glance back into the courtyard where I see three rough-looking middle-aged guys who arrived the day after I did. They wave me over to their table like they want to sell me contraband. Anything to escape the shrewd gaze of the front desk lady and her frustrated authority.

I walk over and rest my hands on the back of the empty chair. "You were wasted the other night, yeah?" says Dave, a flannel-shirt-wearing-self-described-Montana-man. "We saw that blonde girl you brought in here, yeah? You didn't even notice us. I had to show you where your room was, yeah?" This is not from my memory that night, but there are a lot of details misplaced by the alcohol.

"I hope the sex was good, yeah?" This is Dave's big finish and his comrades give up to cheers and back slaps. They laugh and I laugh too, just not on the inside.

"Sit down at the goddamn table and have some lunch with us," says Truck, Dave's childhood friend, who gestures to the bottles on the table. The third member of their trinity, Trent, moves his beer aside to make room for me at the table. He's a truck driver from Wyoming. The three of them are childhood friends who come to Antigua every year around Holy Week to get debauched.

"You're starting early," I tell Trent, noticing the four empty bottles in front of him.

"Well, people's working somewhere. Someone's gotta do it."

They are headed northwest to Lake Atitlán. Dave asks me if I would like to join them, "We're gonna go fishing there, and could use a young guy in the gang to attract some of those pretty, European rainbow trout."

"Maybe you could spawn with them," Trent suggests with a shit-eating grin on his face.

I could do it. I could leave the mess of Antigua behind and start off fresh and new somewhere else—somewhere where no one knows me. But then I imagine that sad look that sometimes appeases in Liam's eyes and think about Stella and for better or worse there are things holding me here. It's not that my life really has more meaning here than it did back home, but I feel like I'm on the brink of finding, I don't know what—purpose? And besides, I would just be a token to these three, existing outside of the bond they spent thirty years forming. So I decline. Dave convinces me to have a beer with them, "You look like hell man, you need a beer. Alcohol can cure anything and the first one's on me." Screw it, I think, and accept his offer.

The front desk woman still looks rather alarmed when I get up and walk past her and out into the street. I take my hand off my stomach and wave it at her, which causes her eyes to widen.

The drone of my stomach: Rabble, rabble, rabble. RABBLE!

The outside light hits squinting pupils that have been raised from the dead. The procession that passed left a trail of rubble and trash everywhere. My lumbering feet, forgetting how to walk, stumble over the uneven cobblestones. Two blocks of walking and I feel exhausted. The street is busy with what appears to be men wearing purple Ku Klux Klan robes. This must be part of the aftermath of the procession that stormed deafeningly by my hostel room a few hours ago.

I try to find an Internet café a block off the Central Park. I haven't contacted my mom since I arrived and she is probably panicking by now. I'm in need of some laundry service too. I soiled my last clean pair of boxers and am now cruising through the streets commando underneath my last pair of clean pants.

Dispersed throughout the Purple People are Mayans wearing colorfully patterned clothing. I had just thought of them as Guatemalans, but now have new eyes to see them.

Some Mayans are begging for change, their dishes extended unbearably away from their bodies.

Here they are. The sons and daughters of kings are begging, letting their blood in the streets. I want to take their dishes and throw them forever far away. I want to shatter their dishes on the stucco walls and tell them to rise up and be the people they know they are. Instinctively my money moves from my pocket, to my hand, to their dishes. They thank me only because they don't know any better. I put an American twenty-dollar bill in one man's pathetic dish. He looks up. His smile seems to drain him of his energy and resign him further to his fate. I keep the secret to myself: charity condemns him. Because where does it end? Where should it end? Who will help him tomorrow when I am not here to feel like shit at having so many somethings when so many have so much nothing? I am helpless in the presence of those who need help. I am helpless.

At the internet café I take a seat among a half-dozen internationals dispersed throughout the computer-filled room. A strange crowd in the age of smartphones; reminds me of the sort of folks who you find at the bus stations in America. A blond, European-looking pervert two computers down from me gestures towards my crotch. I turn from him to my screen. Gesturing like that to a stranger is going too far. From the corner of my eye, I see him continue to make unruly, suggestive gestures towards my inseam.

I open two Internet Explorer windows and direct one to my email account and the other to Facebook. The connection is slow. A blonde American girl in a short skirt is to my right. She's talking loudly into a microphone attached to headphones, "I've completely un-objectified myself!"

I try to keep my gaze on the screen to avoid the depraved eyes of the aggressive homosexual harassing me with tactless advances. Now I understand how women feel when men shamelessly pursue them in public. There is nothing enjoyable about this.

"You could never understand, I am living in a world completely devoid of worldly comforts..." the girl to my right slams a finger down on her computer's keypad.

I have a half dozen notifications on Facebook. I haven't shared with anyone from my former life that I'm in Guatemala, not like any of them would care from the offices where they live their post-graduate lives. I have ten new emails. One is spam—a free Viagra offer. And some Saudi prince has left me millions. Eight emails are from my mom. Each carries an increased worried tone asking if I have arrived safely and how things are. I start a response. Delete. Start again. Delete. Stare at the blank screen.

Totally-un-objectified-girl's volume is increasing, "Yes. Don't worry, his small little opinion has been noted."

I chance a glance over to the blond guy, and when he catches me looking his way he points directly at my crotch and mouths who-knows-what vulgarities. I turn back and the blank screen stares at me and I see a tainted reflection of myself in its glass. I can't read the expression on my face. I notice, disgusted, a few pimples on my right cheek. How old am I? I should be writing an apology to her, but what for? I'm no longer capable of having any idea how my actions translate into other people's lives. I've wronged her in some way I feel, but hasn't she somehow wronged me?

She's only always wanted you to be happy.

Then why is it so hard?

Dear Mom,

Guatemala is great. I really needed to get away and I am glad I am here. You would like it here, lots of Catholic churches everywhere.

Delete, these aren't the words I am looking for. Start again.

Guatemala is great, sorry I didn't write before, I lost my phone and have been enjoying the digital detox. Holy Week started today, but I guess you knew that. My Spanish sucks, but I think I am picking up a little bit here and there. I also have been volunteering at a school for poor kids. You would love this kind of work. Something to put on my résumé when I get back. Maybe it will help me get a job. I hope everything is okay with you. Sorry, I didn't email you sooner. More details coming later. Love, Liam.

Were I to write honestly, I'd write, "I love you" until the screen filled up. Why do I need to be thousands of miles away to realize how incredibly true this is? I would type I-love-yous and only ever stop to fill the screen with thank-yous. I would thank her for loving me and for praying for me, even if those prayers will only ever be a comfort to her.

"It's like, I don't even know how I am going to have normal conversations with people when I get back because they just have no idea about the experiences I have had." Unobjectified-girl rant transports me back to the present.

Gay-blond-European-guy takes the opportunity to point again to my crotch. I log out and get up to leave and he continues to gesture towards my crouch. Oh no. He's getting up. I try to pay, and without waiting for my change, rush to the door. He dashes towards me.

What the hell?
Shit.
Here. He. Comes.
Run.
Rabid Euro-homosexual will never catch me—I will never be had.
FREEDOM!

When he sees that I will evade him, he yells at me in a heavy German accent, "Yoor turtle, yoor littal turtle is hanging owt ov hiz turtle house!"

I look down. My fly is open. My "turtle" is just hanging there for everyone to see.

How long has my penis been poking out?!

The uncomfortable glances of the woman at the front desk make more sense now. I zip up my fly and continue back to Central Park. When I enter the park, I pass a new cluster of beggars. There is this city and its beggars and all over the world beggars are holding out dishes, displaying their amputations for all to see, asking only for enough to live, relying on someone noticing them and showing some mercy. I reach for more money and give them what I find in my pockets. I give my last dirty bunch of Quetzales to a decaying woman hanging her head and clinging to her rag-clothed child. Without looking up or even into her dish, she blesses the air in front of her. Fish for today.

Then the feeling that someone is watching me creeps up like goose bumps. She's there, seated on a park bench. I notice first her single braid intermixed with her other unkempt strands of hair and once again feel certain I know her from somewhere else, somewhere distant and far away from here, but still someplace real. A different voice in my head tells me this is impossible and that it's probably only because she is the first girl since Cathy that I feel something for, but that inner certainty doesn't care about the facts. My stomach strangles itself and I can't tell if this is Stella's fault or if the Mayans are resuming their revenge.

In between a half moon of pigeons, there she is. Both the last and only person I want to see right now. Her long woven skirt is the same sort that the Mayan women wear. Her nose is sunburned, and cheeks burnt the shade of her lips. The birds look up to her expectantly. In half-minute intervals she takes pinches of the seeds and casts it at the mess of them. They trample over each other, grabbing as much as they can. The repetition seems to bore her and she casts volley after volley. Only after one throw hits me in the face do I realize I have been standing staring at her.

Pigeons come racing towards me and peck at my feet as my eyes shut reflexively.

"Aww, you got birdseed in my eyes!"

"Yep, that was the plan. Attack my little palomas, attack the stalker!"

I manage to get one eye working and stumble over the zealous birds.

"You shouldn't throw birdseed at people."

"You shouldn't be a creeper."

"I wasn't being a creeper."

"That's what creepers say."

"Then what do non-creepers say?"

"Non-creepers don't stand there staring."

"I was watching you feed the birds."

"Also known as being a creeper."

My stomach twists and I use all my might to keep my sphincter closed, worried I am about to get incontinent all over these pigeons. The moment passes and I wobble.

"You look like you are going to pass out. Here, sit down." She pats the park bench and I sit down next to her.

"I've been sick for a few days. I think the worst is over though . . ."

"How long have you been here?"

"A week."

"Yeah, it takes a while for your body to adjust to the new bacteria. Evolution never planned on us traveling thousands of miles in a single day in an aluminum tube in the sky. It's unnatural."

"The Mayan's revenge."

"Gross. Why are you out in public?"

"I've been holed up in my hostel forever, this is my feeble attempt at rejoining society. What's with the bird feeding all the time?"

"Birds like to eat. Actually if you want to know a secret," she lowers her voice, "they need to eat."

"What part of the States are you from anyways?" I say, immediately regretting not having something better to ask.

"Jesus my mother!" she says, imitating a Southern accent.

"Your secrecy thing makes you seem like an escaped convict."

"Well, maybe I am. . ." She looks at me playfully from the corner of her eyes and throws another handful of birdseed at my shoes. The birds surround my legs.

"Man, I'm so glad I came out of my sick cave to be abused by a bird lady."

She laughs and smiles and throws the last of her birdseed as far as she can. The pigeons scuttle away to devour the kernels. "Well, I'm getting some coffee. Are you coming?"

My stomach is in no condition to receive coffee, but that's not why I follow. We walk to a café just off the park. I can't understand what she orders because she orders it in fluent Spanish. But I can tell it's elaborate, it takes her a small lifetime to express it to the Guatemalan girl behind the counter. I only know how to say café, so I order that, remembering that I am out of money, devising what I'll do when it's time to pay the tab. The girl behind the counter responds to me in English, "Just a coffee?"

We walk towards a table and I feel triumphant to be sitting with her.

"By the way, I'm Liam," I say.

"Yeah, I know. You told me the last time. For not really wanting to know anything about you, I'm learning a lot." Then she adds, "I know I come across like a bitch to you. The truth is

I am a bitch, so don't take it personally. I'm not an easy nut to crack and all the squirrels go home hungry and disappointed."

"What do you have against squirrels?"

"Pretty much everything. What's not to hate? They are pretentious, the way they strut around with their bushy tails. They are deceitful, with all that nut hiding they do. And they are reckless and that's why they end up as little squirrel pancakes on the road. Don't even get me started on squirrels. They are not cute."

"But pigeons are?"

"Do you know anything about pigeons?"

"Dirty birds that eat garbage in cities?"

She scoffs.

"What's to know then?"

"Where to even begin Aside from the fact that they mate for life, aside from the fact that they saved thousands of lives in World War I, aside from the fact that their poop was an essential resource hundreds of years ago in Europe to make gunpowder, aside from the fact male pigeons can lactate. Did you know that pigeons are the only non-mammal that can recognize themselves in a mirror? Or that they are one of the most intelligent animals on the planet?"

"To me they look like walking soccer balls," I pantomime a kick. She seems about to become violent. I can't tell if she is kidding. I search for something encouraging to say about pigeons, "I guess I never thought much about pigeons, I mean—"

"You mean you have no problem making offhand comments about pigeons even though you've never taken the time to know anything about them?" While I think of a response she jumps back in, "Pound for pound, pigeons are the most intelligent animals in the world. They've been used for communications for longer than, like, anything else. Sikhs feed pigeons for religious reasons. They believe that when they are reincarnated they will never go hungry in their next life if they have fed pigeons in their current life."

"So you feed them to protect your ass in the next life?"

"Maybe. I just want to make sure I got all my bases covered in case the Sikhs are onto something with that."

I want to mention again that I am sure, SURE, that I know her, but I intuitively sense that the second I do, this shred of openness will close, maybe forever. When I imagine telling her that, something she does makes her look so familiar. But I say nothing. Maybe she just has one of those faces. The girl brings us our cafés and we each take an ambitious sip. A lull bubbles up between us and I pop it and say, "So, Quay and the degenerates he hangs with are still planning to do that thing. I tried to talk him out of it, but his mind seems set."

She has a certain way of selecting her words, like before she says something she walks through the whole dictionary, making sure the aptest terms possible are employed. "People who think pain can be cured with more pain are mistaken. But it just means more pain for everyone. The Buddha said that."

She focuses her eyes intently on mine until I blink, "Giving to beggars is one thing, but if you ever want to see the bottom of the world, if you ever want to see the cost of this beautiful life," she pantomimes to her coffee and the chic café we're seated in, "If you ever want to really get it, go to El Basurero in Cuidad Vieja."

She studies me to see if I've understood. "El ba-sur-ero. It means dump. Will you remember?"

I tell her I will, but really am debating if I should tell her that I think it was Quay who bought the bad cocaine for Shannon, wondering if this will change how she sees it, not sure if this changes how I see it. But I settle for something neutral, "How did you meet Quay and stuff?"

She reaches and places her hand atop mine, "Promise me before you leave Guatemala you will go there?"

This moment might go on to be the most intimate we ever share, but who knows, the future is unwritten.

I tell her I will and she releases my hand and says, "Look Liam, there are two kinds of foreigners in this town. The ones who are here for a nice vacation, like you, and the ones who have been here too long, like Quay. The ones who have been here too long all end up falling into each other, and here you can become best friends without knowing anything about someone. I have known who Quay is for maybe a year, but I couldn't tell you his last name, or where he's from, or what his favorite animal is, or why he's a douche bag. This is a town of drunks and volunteers, retirees, vagabonds, ramblers, people 'saving the world,' run-away artists, and people who used to save the world but now are jaded and broken and hate the world but love scotch and whiskey, and people who are just like, lost, and junkies wanting a cheap score, and people who are all of these things. And the best thing about this crazy lot and is that no one cares who or what you were or are outside of here because everyone is so busy living out their own narcissistic dreams and addictions and getting drunk and high that they really don't have time to care too much time to judge you or pin you into a consistent personality. Get it?"

I ask her how long she's been in Guatemala and somehow this question is too much for me to get a straight answer. She shows something between pity and joviality, and stirs more sugar into her coffee. "Don't you even put any sugar in your coffee?"

"I like my coffee like I like my women, black and strong," I smile broadly.

"I try not taste any coffee," she says adding more sugars.

I steer the conversation back to my question, "Well, everyone else I meet seems to be open about where they're from and what they're doing. Maybe it's you who are off on your own adventure and don't have time to focus on anyone else's."

Her pupils contract as her eyes grow big. She taps her spoon on the side of her mug, "I lead my life a certain way for certain reasons. Let's just leave it at that. I've been here too long, and before here I was somewhere else too long and I bet when I leave here I'll be somewhere else too long. You got it?"

For no reason she smacks me hard in the shoulder and my whole arm tingles. Then I laugh. Maybe I'm laughing at how hard I am trying to bring this conversation where it will not go, or how much I am failing to connect with her, or because right now my high school friend is plotting to kill someone, or it could be how sick the coffee is making my poor stomach feel, and maybe it's the walking around half the morning with my penis hanging out of my pants, or my mom praying for me as if I need help from the culprit of it all, or living off of money from my dead dad's car. Whatever it is, something suddenly seems hilarious.

She glares, sensing that this laughter is from an inside joke she is outside of. I give up on laughter and push the conversation forward with every bit of sociability I have,

"Okay, how about at least tell me where you've been? For research, I'm interested in going other places and I need to know whether or not they suck."

Some of her secrecy softens. "Everywhere sucks if you suck. So I'd worry more about the traveler than where he travels. But I did a year in Asia. Africa. Europe, but that's so expensive, so that means it sucks for you if you're broke. I spent a year in Colombia, and I was all over South America."

As she names off places, I see them on a map in my mind. My older brother and I used to take turns closing our eyes and spinning a globe with a finger on it. Wherever our finger landed was where we were going to live one day. Usually, we lived in the ocean. When did I stop seeing the world as this accessible?

"You guys impress me," I tell her.

"What do you mean you guys?"

"You know—you guys— travelers who aren't just taking a trip. Here I feel like I'm trying to take a test without reading the book. Unless you count Canada, this is my first real trip out of the country. When I'm around you guys, I feel like you all know what the hell you're doing here."

She laughs in a high pitch and looks as if to say that there's more to learn than I ever will. "The people who inspire you are a pretty miserable lot mate. It starts innocent enough, with just one plane ticket. But then you see the people who have been on the road for decades who seem so lost and can't tell the difference between their ideals and the ghosts of their ideals. At a certain point everyone should just go home and get a job. "

"Are you including yourself in that?"

"I'm not everyone."

"Who are you then?"

She hesitates, "I guess I just try to convince myself I'm not like everyone else... Maybe in a way we're all after the same thing."

"Being?" Her face changes from light and graceful to serious and speculative.

"It must be the answer to that question. Because if we knew what we were looking for, we'd at least know when we'd found it. But I think knowing it is also finding it, you know?"

She shrugs and takes it somewhere else, "But in the shear practicality of life on the road, if you stay too long around the same people, they expect you to be a certain way. So you're stuck being that person. Gets pretty hectic, don't you think?" She looks at me, wondering if I understand what she's trying to say. I do, of course, finally hearing it expressed so simply the reason I came.

"So," I venture, breaking what could have been a long time wordlessly facing each other, "How do you know when it's time to go?"

The moment vanishes, "When you know, you go, you know?"

"But how do you *know*?"

We let the question float away and attend to our beverages. I replay what she said in my mind. I want it to be that simple and unfair. So many people tried to help me, tried to change me. But it's only now that I've escaped from their censuring eyes that I feel I've started to regain lost bits of who I was. I wonder if I could have done that with them.

She inhales her coffee, "So, since you're so eager to pry into my personal life, let's hear a little about you. The game is a give and take kinda game, you know?"

I shake my head. "Mine's not really the kind you tell."

She swirls a straw around her drink. "Either everyone's story is worth hearing or no one's is. L

"Does this apply to your story too?"

She disarms me with a glance. I try to find a place to start. "Well, I'm from Eugene. It's in Oregon."

And I begin to hear my voice tell a story that I've never heard before. I relive it in my mind every day, and sometimes share certain details of it, but I've never really tried to fit all these jagged pieces together. Not like this anyway. It's like someone else's story—the story of things that happened to someone, not a story of me happening to things. I want to be Timmy or Tommy. Their lives are worth it. Their stories are their stories.

There are certain moments I remember, but only as the final number and not the equation that led to it. I don't start at the beginning, but the moment I realized just how to shit everything was going and how helpless I was to stop it.

According to everyone else, Cathy was perfect for me. Even before the funerals, she was great in ways I didn't know someone could be. When both funerals had run their course and the tombstones were paid for, she was patient, but cautious and tried to do whatever it was she thought she needed to. Hers must have been a different hell from mine—a helpless hell.

"I was cruel to her after that," I tell Stella, realizing for the first time I was not the only victim. She must have been trying so hard to help me put the pieces back together. She told me that life would go on in careful, kind ways and when it didn't. I blamed her for lying to me. 'You'll get through this', she said. 'I understand,' she said. But we didn't get through it. Not together. And I avoided her because I couldn't bear her happiness. I didn't want to feel better. I needed to be broken. For Dad and Chris. 'I'm gonna make you feel better,' she said. 'I'm going to cook for you, we'll have wine, and candles, and I am yours all night.'

It had been almost six months since the second tombstone and people were less and less understanding of the way I was. I just couldn't walk down perfect paths in my mind when all I wanted to do was break dishes. Candlelight dancing around her smile—the smell of chicken parmesan and the bite of chardonnay—her laughter floating around the room—both of us there for the other—the bedroom in her apartment with scented candles burning—her looking at me with that smile that made me hate her—that sweet flirtatiousness. She did all this for me; despite everything she saw, all this for me. She was always so happy. Nothing, not even my cruelty, seemed to faze her. And everything would have been perfect and beautiful. But that's not what I wanted. I just wanted to smash plates and swallow the shards and feel them cut through my insides.

She told me that she would pick me up at 6 p.m. There was no way I was going to show up sober and I didn't have anything to drink at my apartment so I went to the Missile Toe. It was 4 p.m. After several whiskey cokes, things started to become clear, so I ordered more. I did not need anyone. That was the problem. You think you need people and that dependency causes every imaginable stress. Pain comes from attachments. Lose attachments and pain loses its grip.

My friends started showing up. This was the bar where everyone used to go. Lisa and Tom were the first to show up.

They were excited to see me and pulled up stools to my right. There are some couples, so completely attached, that they have forgotten that life is possible without the other, and cannot stand to be outside of each others' arms. Tom and Lisa were like this.

"You alright, Lee?" Lisa asked me.

"I hate people that ask questions like that," I replied.

Tom did not know I was telling her off. He just laughed and said that he enjoyed my dry sense of humor. Then came Teddy and Bill. They were always together and perpetually loud. They bought me a drink.

"Is this just a coke?"

"No, it's a whiskey coke."

"So they serve whiskey in plastic cups now?" I was angry.

Bill came close and whispered in my ear, "Take it slow man, you have all night. We don't want to lose you before midnight." This was all for show, I thought, thinking that everyone came here to whisper and laugh behind my back.

My phone kept ringing, just as fast as I could ignore her calls.

"How dare he order me a coke and tell me it's a whiskey coke. Does he think I'm seventeen?" I told Teddy, wishing he was as concerned about Bill's behavior as I was.

Then came Mark and Heather, "Leester, what is up? Didn't you have something with Cathy tonight? She called me asking if I knew where you were."

"Hey, Mark, why don't you worry about your own girlfriend and let me worry about mine."

Heather thought this was funny. She laughed, begging me to continue. Everyone else was laughing, so I gave them more of what they wanted. "I'm actually really surprised you and Heather have made it this long. I remember the night you met her, you said she wasn't that good looking, but she looked like an easy lay." I was not making anything up, only repeating what he had actually said.

Bill tried to pull me away, "Let's play darts, Liam."

I could not take the patronizing, but worse was everyone's unanimous insistence that no one was patronizing anyone. "Yeah we can play darts, but after I tell Tom the story about how you banged his girlfriend the week before they started dating, ever tell him that Heather?"

Bill slid closer to me. My phone rang again. Ignore. Mark grabbed my arm and pulled me off the barstool. It's hard to focus on anything when people are shouting in your face. It's harder to pay attention when they say things like, "It's eight-fucking-thirty and you're like this a-fucking-gain. Everyone is tired of your bullshit. You understand? We've all had it. And don't say what you're about to say. This shit started happening before all that. I know. I was there. You gotta get yourself together."

The doors opened and closed. Cathy walked in and took a deep breath. She walked right past me and Mark. Mark was still grabbing my collar. Everyone else in the bar was looking at us. The music still played, but no one could hear it. Cathy was wearing a jean jacket and a blue scarf. Looking completely composed, she sat down at the bar and ordered something. Seeing her determination, I knew.

Mark let my collar go. "She's been calling and texting me for the last hour wondering where the hell you are. You better go talk to her if you haven't already ruined this for yourself."

And there I was, standing alone in the middle of the bar. Cathy with her back to me. Everything perfectly clear. Decided. These people were not my friends. I wanted to grab their shoulders and shake them until they understood. Listen to me! I wanted to say. But none of them would have understood. How could Cathy have just sat their ignoring me like that? Without even hearing my side of the story. I needed to go, but I couldn't go without Cathy. But she was turned away from me. I did not know that I had shouted something until Mark grabbed my shoulders and shouted, "Don't you dare yell at her."

My memory dies here. Other things may have happened or been said before I went to the door, but all I remember was rushing to the door to leave. I tried to slam it when I left, but it was on a hydraulic hinge. I pulled something in my shoulder in the attempt. The air outside was cruel. A cold drizzle attacked me from every side. I stood outside the bar shivering, waiting to see who would come out and what they would have to say. No one came out. No one had anything to say and this just proved that I had been right about them all. Not my friends.

I waited between minutes and hours. Every time the door opened I expected it to be one of them. Strangers walked in and out. And that's what they were, strangers. They were strangers who stayed in the bar. I looked at my phone for missed calls and texts. I found neither. Not even from Cathy. Just nothing. So I hurled my phone to the ground and watched with satisfaction when it broke into a dozen useless pieces. Then I stomped home through the drizzle until I was numb to it. Mark didn't come home that night. And four months later he moved in with Heather. And now it's five months later and I'm here. There's not much to tell after this.

I tell Stella about my brother and dad and mom, her religion, and avoiding every specific detail I can, what killed them. I don't care why I feel so comfortable telling all of this to someone who is basically a stranger, because I can't imagine telling it like this to anyone else. When I finish, I'm left with half a cup of cold coffee, feeling that I am not myself, that this person was lost, has left, and the story stuck in the space behind my eyes is waste that someone else dumped inside me.

When she sees I have nothing more to say she blurts out, "That's kinda bullshit."

I nod, glad that she agrees and take a sip of my cold coffee.

"No," she corrects, "I mean the way you tell your story is bullshit."

"What? I didn't make anything up."

"Yeah," she gives me a distant look and is smiling as if she is about to explain to a five-year-old where babies really come from. "But you didn't tell me anything good. Your life hasn't been all bad."

She transforms a deep breath into a sigh. "Your story went from one pity line to another. You have had like what, maybe a half-hour of actually really, really bad moments. You found out that your dad died in like what? Fifteen seconds? Same with your brother. You have a half-hour, at most, of tragedy in your life, and you just filled the twenty minutes you had to tell your story with all that—like your life has been one continuous tragedy. I asked you about you, not a laundry list of everything that's gone wrong. Jesus my mother."

My wordless mouth opens, but before I can say anything she leans closer and fills the silence. "You're sitting with a girl who wants to talk to you. Give me something to feel for you other than pity."

She dismisses me with a wave of a mean hand. "I'm gonna go order another coffee. Let me know if you are still going to be telling your tear jerkers when I get back, so I can have her put rum in it."

As she leaves me alone with my thoughts. I can do nothing but watch Stella explain her eccentrically long coffee order to the barista behind the counter. While she prepares the coffee they chat lightly, both laughing on cue. When both coffees are ready, she thanks the girl by placing her hand atop hers and pays our tab.

She returns and sets a steaming coffee in front of me and holds onto the handle of an elaborate drink topped with whip cream and sprinkles.

There is nothing I can say. No way to return to the light conversation we tossed backed and forth only minutes ago. I take a sip of the new coffee and burn my tongue. This new pain makes me notice the cramps in my stomach have disappeared. My mind is always filled with so many things I can't express. I want to retell my story until we both understand. I want to shout my story until I tell it right. So she can see it through my eyes and feel it through my stomach. I burn my tongue again but don't fucking care. I relish the feeling of scalding coffee cooking my throat. Bloodletting. All this is how some other story begins, and I have no idea if that story will be a happy or sad story and if it will be my story or someone else's.

I put my hands behind my head. "Whatever, I told you, I haven't told anyone and that wasn't easy. At least I had the guts to tell it."

She exhales noisily, "I came here to get coffee with you. So no, I don't have to do anything more than drink coffee. Let people come to you, don't demand things from them. You should really be paying me for this. Lots of therapists make good money listening to stories like yours."

"Maybe we should just go back to talking about your pigeons and their gun powder shit?" I meant to say this nastily, but it seems I've missed the malicious mark. She touches my hand like she did before, and that lifts me out. Everything that needed to happen to lead to this moment, dark or light, seems acceptable since it led me to exactly this spot with her hand on top of mine.

When she removes her hand to join the other that's embracing her mug, I say, "Screw the past then. What about the future. What do you want to do in the future?"

"To always be as happy as I am now."

I place my finger in my coffee to see if it has cooled down, "How happy are you right now?"

She shows me her teeth. "The happiest I have ever been."

"Happier than yesterday?"

"Oh yes, much happier than yesterday."

"But what do you like, want to do specifically with all this happiness?"

"Specifically," she pauses after every syllable, "I want to always be this happy or happier. I want to wake up in the morning and make it to the night and feed lots of pigeons along the way. And drink coffee with lots of cream and sugar and sprinkles and live in a castle made of frosting and raise a family of snow children. Because frosting and sprinkles taste like happiness. So, I want to feed pigeons, drink lots of coffee, and be happy. Got it?" She takes in a long drink and an exaggerated breath blows a sustained sigh into my face, "Can you feel all the bliss in there?"

"Are you on Facebook?"

"Facebook is better left in the hand stalkers like you."

"Don't you want to keep track of all the awesome stalkers you meet along the way?" I raise my eyebrows and point to myself.

"Gross. I don't need any more excess baggage. My pack's h-e-a-v-y."

"There's no way you plan on being like this forever. You'll settle down somewhere, sometime."

"I'm glad you have my personal choices planned out for me. Once I see where a road leads, I lose the desire to go there. I'd rather walk into darkness because it could be anything. Nothing illuminated has ever really interested me."

The conversation continues through Stella buying us third and fourth cups of coffee, which is a new form of excess

I hadn't yet known. When my hands tremble from the caffeine, I forget to be awkward and she forgets to be standoffish. Effortlessly she is witty and wonderful—the kind of person that makes you glad there are people. It's dark when we leave the café. Beneath the nocturnal curtain, I ask her if she wants to grab a beer with me or get some dinner, but she tells me to go home and go to bed unless I want another week of "Mayan" diarrhea.

"But tell you what," she says, seeing the hope flicker out of my face, "Every Saturday I make stir fry at my apartment. We can meet at the bar I met you at 7 pm, then we can watch the Saturday procession before." Her eyes focus on the corner of the room, "The Holy Saturday procession isn't like the other ones. It's dark and amazing."

When we part and I walk back to the hostel, I see something about the beggars I didn't before. There's a sorta joy there. They live off of kindness, and everyday people reach out and give them that.

Things are as good as they get for one day. I drift in and out of a light sleep that I wake from it smiling. Smiling because tomorrow is Monday. Then will come Tuesday. Then it will be Saturday. Smiling because now she's more than a strange familiarity that makes me believe we are somehow interwoven into each other. It was a good day. And all my tomorrows are coming right up and newly limitless. She's made me feel honest and innocent in the face of whatever shit things the world might still be planning for me.

My dreams are filled with chopsticks and her face which inspires something like courage in me. I need to bring chopsticks. But that won't be enough. I need to be able to tell her that I stopped it all, that I convinced Quay not to go through with this moronic plan. Awake beneath the blanket, I repeat the fantasy until it feels possible, and instead of dreaming, I start planning, wondering how she would see me if I succeeded.

CHAPTER EIGHTEEN

The kids begin to arrive. It's a short week for them. Wednesday at noon they're off for Easter vacation. The anticipation turns all their dials up. A little girl runs up to me and hugs my legs. I don't recognize her but she greets me by name. I lift her up and she screams and laughs as I maneuver her through the air. Her smile is missing its front teeth. I try to set her down, but she holds her arms up to me making little pleading hops. We both speak the language of kids flying through the air. Other students see this and run up to me, demanding to be lifted up. One of them picks up the broom I have discarded and resumes sweeping. Well, he's not really sweeping, he's beating the ground with it and occasionally looking up at me for approval. I lift the clamoring kids and swing them through the air until a ringing bell makes them disappear around the corner to line up before going together to breakfast. But the first little girl doesn't leave. She hides behind my legs until her teacher comes to pull her away. She gives me an embarrassed and exasperated smile.

"*Vamos Mercedes*," her teacher says, gently leading her by the hand. But Mercedes breaks free and gives me a final hug before being led away.

Pablo walks up from behind me accompanied by someone. "They are good childrens. And you bring them joy. The girl you throw up first, she was happy. She once live in a garbage dump collecting bottles. But now no. Now she is in school. This is better."

Remembering the person next to him, Pablo puts his hand on his shoulder, "He is Julio. He is my brother."

Julio shakes his head and says in Spanish that seems to contradict whatever Pablo said.

"Okay," Pablo laughs, "We are not brothers. Not really, but we are like brothers. We grow up in the same orphanage for kids when their parents die in the war."

Just then Quay strolls out of a classroom and says good morning. "How are you feeling?" he asks, and I'm glad he's only asking about my stomach. I tell him that I'm feeling better. Julio shakes my hand and excuses himself.

"I was thinking," I tell Quay, "We should cook some dinner at your place soon."

"Tonight I don't think so," He says, "But we could do tomorrow. Or better yet. Thursday. Holy Thursday." I search his face for a sign that the schedule conflict is not the deed. I find nothing.

So I tell him, "Okay, let's do Thursday. Quay returns to the classroom and Pablo returns to ask me, "So, what it means when you say, 'you are breaking my balls?"

I laugh at his eager face. "It means like, you're bothering me."

He nods. "So," he continues, "what does it mean when they say 'you can have my sloppy seconds?'"

"Pablo, where did you learn all these?"

"My friend tells them to me."

"This guy doesn't sound like your friend."

Pablo is unfazed and continues to fire off an accumulation of English confusion my way. The conversation continues this way until I jump in with,

"When are you doing it? "

Pablo understands what "it" signifies and his face drops.

"Tomorrow?" I ask.

"No."

"When then?"

"Saturday."

"Holy Saturday?" I say with the sort of indignation one holds for the violated sacred. That ends our language exes for and for the rest of the morning we work in silence. We clean bathrooms and wash the morning's dishes, side by side, both thinking the same thought from different places.

Then something alights in Pablo, "Hey after work you want to play music with me? I play guitar with some friends who plan drums."

"I don't play anything," I say simply.

"It is okay," Pablo says. But I say nothing more and I don't know what Pablo did to me to deserve that. Whatever it is, it does not seem okay.

CHAPTER NINETEEN

I was scheduled to come back after lunch to volunteer at the school, but I don't show up. It's not a real job, just tasks invented for me so I can feel like I'm making the difference I'm not. At the hostel I eat lunch without feeling any hunger for it. A dozen people are sitting at the three little tables in the courtyard. Somehow, I've ended up at a table with a lunatic.

"I'm somewhat of a sexual revolutionary," the skinny, middle-aged man in front of me in skimpy cutoff jean shorts explains to me. His voice crescendos as his finger rises, "STDS are a myth. Plain and simple!"

I ignore him, but that seems to only give him more permission. "I started the nudist movement as it exists today," he says, spitting as he does. His yellow eyes suggest he's been up since the night before. He scratches his nose like he's trying to remove it. How is it this was the only open seat in the hostel restaurant? My steak sandwich tastes like shameful embarrassment. Girls are looking at me, unpleased.

"If you're a nudist, then why are you wearing clothes?" I ask him the stupidest possible question to ask an alleged nudist. Wheels are set in motion. He takes his shirt off, exposing his wrinkling body and gray chest. There is a tattoo of a dolphin riding a unicorn across his left peck. He nods in a didn't-I-tell-you type way. People around us pause mid-conversation to watch the stripping man.

But even though he's right in front of me, he feels as far away as the world I left behind. I'm thinking about Stella. What is it about her and what about everybody else in the world? He's down to his whitey-tighty Fruit of the Looms. From their coloration, it seems the banana has gone bad. I am thankful and surprised he is wearing underwear. I cram the rest of my lunch into my mouth.

"What has changed here?" he gestures to his flabby, bare chest.

"You're no longer wearing a shirt," I offer. "And you took off your pants."

"Ah, yes, but what has really changed?" He raises his eyebrows.

"Your shirt and pants. They are now covering my basket of tortillas instead of on you, where they should be. That has changed and it makes everyone very uncomfortable."

"Yes, but nothing about us here in this moment has changed." He fiddles with the fly of his underwear. He plays with the elastic band, threateningly. A giggle or a gasp comes from across the room. People are looking, pretending they aren't. I should just leave, but cannot tear myself away from this. Now I just need to know what will happen. Will he or won't he bust it out? Lively conversations have diminished to a dubious murmur. Everyone is watching, needing to know if he will. He extends his tanned arms in Christlike fashion for everyone in the room to behold him. But he is looking at me.

"Tell me?" He breaks wind loudly and a girl at the table next to us loudly lifts her plate and walks to her room, "What has really changed here?"

There is still a pile of fries on my plate, but I abandon them and stand up. I am no longer hungry. No one is. A few hostel-goers are still fixated. He has them as they watch him teeter over the edge. He glances at his body and comments in the voice of vindication. "I am the way nature intended me to be. I am natural. I am free."

"You're right," I say not looking, but knowing what he's done, "Nothing has changed. Except now you're eating alone." I had been practicing this comeback for a few minutes, editing it, swapping out words until it was just right. Just another crazy in this wildly mad world.

I head to my room. There are so many things I should be doing—the things that everyone else in this hostel talks about doing. Climbing the volcano Pacaya, enrolling for a few days in a Spanish school, seeing Lake Atitlan, traveling around the country. But Antigua has strong arms and right now she has me. I'm stuck in some sort of suspended animation surrounding what Quay does and how I might stop him. But is it really about that? Or is it because of Stella I'm staying around? I want to be like the sane travelers I see, out exploring, having fun. But really, I see that I only want to want this, but don't really care.

I go out and buy a loaf of bread and then walk towards the wine shop where Stella works. It might be better to wait till Saturday. But there are a million mights. One 'might' is to go to her right now and this might be the best might of them all. I pass the church La Merced on the way. Its yellow façade rises above the mortals below. I glimpse just how temporary everything really is in the face of stone walls reaching above the city, across centuries.

My mind wakes back up and starts to worry about every possibility it can summon. I tell it to shut up. When it does not, I walk inside the church and kneel in one of the pews. It does not mean or change anything, but I understand something now. I understand the need for this. I need this right now because there is a wine shop filled with Stella mixed with what are the odds of me stopping Quay? I crash between confidence and the certainty that I will fail, which is still easier than to think about than wondering how my world would look and what life would be like if everything worked out.

So I pray to pass the time. I pray because I have nothing better to do. I pray almost forgotten words and wonder if my mom is chanting the same prayers for a much different reason a world away. In front of me is a dead man. I look up and see him hanging from a cross and wonder if he would have ever dreamed that two thousand years later someone like me would be kneeling in front of him. And maybe he did not believe his claim either. Maybe everyone just misunderstood. Maybe he misled them so they'd listen. Maybe he knew that his message would have never been accepted if people thought that it was coming from a mere man. So I pray to the dead man, not because I think he can hear me, but because it makes me feel less alone.

The door to the shop is open. Stella is putting a bottle into a bag and giving it to a man. I wait until he leaves and watch her sit back down at the big glass table. Strewn about in front of her are loose sheets of paper with sketches drawn on them. I swallow and walk forward. Does she look happy to see me?

"Hey," her smile signals my relieving sigh, "I was actually just thinking about you. You're not allergic to anything are you?"

"Only poison and rattlesnake venom."

"Shit, that rattlesnake venom hot sauce was expensive!"

"I have something for you," I say, producing the loaf of bread, "I didn't know where to find birdseed for your winged friends. But they'll like this. It's whole wheat. Healthy."

"I haven't taken my break yet, so as long as you feed me too, I can slip away with you for a few."

She gathers the sketches and places them in her purse. We walk out to the cobblestone streets and my impromptu visit is as perfect as I hoped it would be. I am reminded of that first night when she walked into the bar and I don't have to wonder anymore where I know her from. I know her from Guatemala. I know her from the park where we drink coffee and feed birds. And if we can do this, we could be more, and if we can do that, then what's to ever stop us?

After Cathy, I thought that was it. When a relationship ends, it feels so final—you are sure that expired feeling will never be felt for someone again. Then you board a plane, fulfilling the absurd dream of flight, meet someone, and bam, the feeling's right there where you left it. And you feel it when that someone walks into the street with you in a blue sundress with that single braid mixed up with her bangs, tied with a sea-green ribbon.

You feel it when she reaches for your arm and you walk with her arm and arm into the park and she is confident or maybe just as nervous and pretending, like me, to be sure of herself.

I look at her and I see an un-lived future is excruciating because any minute, it could be decided. She asks how much longer I am going to be in Antigua. The question catches me off guard. My life in Eugene seems distant and past. I tell her that like her, I'm not sure. Maybe right now. Maybe tomorrow. Maybe a week from now. Or maybe never. People do this all the time. They disappear from their old lives and reappear into other people's. I could get a job down here, or go with her if she leaves.

She stops and buys coffee and a bagel. I stand in her way and pay.

"I have to tell you about my lunch." I use my body as a model to explain in intricate detail the nearly naked man's antics at my table. She laughs so hard that she snaps her fingers to the rhythm of the hilarity. The worst song that could possibly be stuck in my head is playing on repeat. The crab from The Little

Mermaid is singing to me. I don't want him to. I want him to shut up. He's telling me to kiss Stella.

"It's not as bad as this customer at the wine shop this morning," she says. "He was wearing jean cutoffs, smelled like a rotting mango, and spat his tobacco on the floor. Just hawked it up and spat. I wasn't even angry, just like, in awe of him."

Once we're set up on a park bench, I break my bread into tiny morsels and throw them to the eager birds. "It's kinda relaxing, feeding pigeons. There's a rhythm to it."

"It makes you feel like a god," she says, flicking crumbs with her tiny fingers. "And I'm an unjust one. I always choose some pigeons over others."

The pigeons dance wherever our tosses direct them.

"So," she pauses from feeding the frenzy, "I technically don't get like a lunch break. I'm allowed to close the shop for a little bit while I grab something to eat there."

"Well, if you want I can just go back there and taste wine all afternoon with you."

"No way José. I not going to hang out someone getting loaded unless I can get loaded too."

"Or you could just blow off work and we could get loaded here in the park," I say listening to the playfully falling water of the fountain. "I could sit here all day."

She blushes for the first time for me to see, and she doesn't respond with anything to take away from what I've just said. I should just kiss her now, then I'd know one way or another. I could wait, but time could ruin things. Time always finds a way to mess things up.

A little boy saves me. He comes up and asks if we would like our shoes shined. Stella declines, but pats the park bench for him to sit down next to us. She re-opens the bag of bread and hands him a slice, instructing him in the art of feeding the pigeons. He shoves the first slice into his mouth. Stella laughs and shows him how to throw pieces of bread to the birds. He tears his second slice in half, giving the bigger piece to the birds. Laughing at how the birds fight over the piece of bread he's thrown to them. Stella scoops him up and puts him on her lap and hands him another slice to throw. I would've guessed he was nine years old, but now on Stella's lap, he seems younger. With each throw he shakes with excitement, his shoeshine kit forgotten, he's been permitted to be a kid again.

"His name is Josè," Stella tells me, putting him back on the bench. She moves closer to me until she's leaning against me. She says some words in Spanish to the little boy which makes him laugh and at every pause turns to me so that we can share in the mirth. When the last slice of bread has been given to the birds, she hugs the boy and slides a five Quetzal bill into his hands. He picks up his small wooden shoeshine kit from the ground and waddles away in search of shoes in need of shining.

"That was nice," I tell her.

She beams and closes her eyes while breathing in the afternoon air. Her head seems about to rest on my shoulder, but instead, she rises and brushes off the crumbs covering her skirt, "Yes, this was nice. I wish I could stay longer, but I gotta get back to the shop. If I don't see you before then, I'll see you Saturday 7 pm. Don't be late. And bring something." lol She kisses me on the cheek and then hugs me, holding me longer than someone who was just a friend would.

Back at the hostel I ADHD my way through activities that don't hold my attention. I try reading, but toss my book down on a hammock and walk around aimlessly. There are a half dozen people in the courtyard, reading, talking, smoking weed, hanging out. Most of them greet me, some by name. I think about ordering a beer and wonder if I'm hungry. A recklessly tanned guy wearing sandals and cut-off camouflage shorts walks in with an enormous backpack weighing him down.

My mind flashes to my brother Chris. Camouflage, embarrassment, Chris's laugh and smile, the way he mowed the lawn without his shirt on, his endless dedication to fitness and eating right, wearing his army fatigues when he didn't need to, embarrassing me in public since I was the guy hanging out with G.I. Joe. I never told him I was embarrassed about that because deep down I knew I should have been proud of him.

"Interesting take on things," he had told me when I showed him a college paper I had written titled: Evil Men Start Wars, Virtuous Men Fight Them. My premise was that blind obedience to country, the sense of patriotic duty, was what allowed war. That if soldiers everywhere decided their own lives were more important than fighting wars, there wouldn't be wars. If soldiers threw down their weapons, peace would be inevitable. The paper was the typical sort written by first-year college students flying high on untested ideals. I don't know why I showed it to Chris or what sort of response I was hoping for from a soldier. He was gracious to me and my rants.

Maybe I had hoped for some admittance that it was soldiers like him who allowed war. Maybe I wanted him to actually argue his side instead of dismissing mine. Maybe I wanted him to admit he was a moron for joining the army. But really, I think I was just terrified that he wasn't going to come home.

I ADHD my way out of the hostel and walk across Antigua's uneven cobblestones. Time has become eternal and the world uninteresting. At every intersection there are three forward choices and one backward. There are still several hours of daylight.

In an Internet café, I make sure that my turtle is safely tucked away. I log onto Facebook and my Hotmail account. There's an email from my mom, she's happy that I am having fun. I respond to my mom with a light message about how I'm enjoying my time volunteering and just being here in general. I think about mentioning Stella, or anything specific, but then hit the send button and watch my message magically disappear. Plenty of spam has made it through my useless spam filter. They are offering me free Viagra and some Saudi Prince has left me millions.

Leaving, I remember that I need to find chopsticks. Where am I going to get chopsticks in Latin America? What if I succeed? What if Stella wants me to kiss her? I imagine the inside of her apartment is cozy, with a small couch, a crackling fire, weathered tapestries adorning the castle wall my mind creates. I bet her books are stacked on the floor instead of on shelves. I imagine when we eat dinner we sit on a loveseat over the coffee table since that's the only seat other than the bed, which I imagine to be in the same room of what has gone from a castle to a studio apartment. We can't stop laughing as we chopstick food into our mouths. A bottle of wine is between us. Or maybe it's a bottle of saki. Afterward we take our dishes to the kitchenette and seat ourselves on her bed where we listen to light acoustic music, each with a glass of wine in hand, each laughing at the other's hilarity. Then we kiss. Then we hold each other. Then our bodies instinctively begin a dance that ends with. . . And then the fantasy fades away and the reality around me returns. I'm not hopeless or helpless. I can change. I can evolve. It's not about wanting to have sex with Stella. But when a woman invites you over for dinner is it ever about dinner?

My will-not-shut-up mind will do what it always does: sabotage me, frighten me with its incessant imagined fears. Eventually i's always about sex. No matter how people say it isn't, it always, always, always is. It's not that I want to have sex with her. It's not that I don't want to either. But if things work out, that's an essential part of the dance. Until sex is settled, everyone is holding their breath.

CHAPTER TWENTY

"Do you ever eat anything else?"

Quay leans over the popping skillet in front of him. "Why would I?"

"For the sheer thrill of change" My beer is warm and I don't want to finish it.

"I say once you find a food that works, stick with it." He flips the frying slab of meat and turns the blue flame down.

"Doesn't that get expensive?"

"Not if you buy it in bulk from the market. There's half a cow in my freezer."

I'm sitting on the counter as Quay attends to the sizzling meat. To pass the time I'm creating different geometric patterns in my mind by seeing the lines between the cinderblocks composing the wall.

Quay puts a cover on the skillet and pulls plastic jars of seasoning out from the cupboard. He catches me out of the corner of his eye, "I never asked you how things panned out with you and the Swedish chick."

The pyramid pattern I just conjured disappears back into the wall. Quay stands like an idiot in front of the opened cupboard door, looking expectantly at me. Without lying, I say, "If you are wondering if we went back to my hostel and got naked, the answer is yes."

He whistles softly, "And you're staying in the dorms,"

"Yep, in a dorm room."

He whistles again, "I bet you are a popular guy at the hostel."

"Everyone was asleep."

"Doubtful."

"Weren't you sneaking out with the other one, Karen or whatever?"

His smile tells me I'm not going to like whatever he is about to say, ``A gentleman never asks; a woman never tells."

I take a moment to solve the puzzle and, "So if you don't tell, that makes you a woman, right?"

"I've changed a lot since high school, you know." He takes off the lid and sprinkles a healthy dose of something over the nearly finished steak.

"Who hasn't?"

"I feel like most people just followed the script: college, job, marriage, kids."

"So what?"

"And that wasn't for me."

"Well, doing what you're doing... that probably isn't for them."

"You got that right." Quay turns off the burner. It's just us here. He's already shown me his life, explained to me his dreams and his motivations behind them, and for a moment it seems he's just another human, another broken person muddling through life. This Quay is the Quay worth knowing.

When it's time to eat we ignore the table. Instead we surround the skillet like a pair of wolves who have just taken down our prey. Each armed with a knife and fork, we hover over the steak-filled skillet and cut fat chunks off the slab of meat in front of us. Quay walks over to the fridge and sets a fresh beer in front of me, even though I still have half of my last one left.

"You seem to be getting along with the kids at my school," he says, choking on his steak.

The image of Mercedes running from her teacher to give me a final hug returns. "I like being there. I haven't been around kids since I was a kid. I had forgotten how happy they are, like, all the time. And when I hear about some of the shit those kids have lived through, damn. How the hell are they still able to run and laugh and enjoy life as much as they do?"

"I wonder why we lose that," Quay says more to himself than to me.

"Maybe around the time we realize it's not all happily ever after, that bad things happen to good people, life doesn't turn out the way it should, and we're all on a one-way track speeding towards our death."

"Great Liam—a really valuable perspective worth sharing you got there," he chews another hunk off the slab on his fork and continues, "Some of these kids... Well, you know... you know that some of them were trafficking victims, forced to work, some of the older ones were forced to work as prostitutes, and when you're around that every day it starts to eat away at everything. You ask yourself things like, 'How can I go to an art gallery and look at paintings that are pointless while children a few miles away are starving to death or being beaten and trafficked?' Everything loses its luster. You feel guilty if you go to the movies, or enjoy a nice meal, or drink a beer, or read a book. You wonder, 'how the hell can I enjoy these trivial things when there are lives being crushed everywhere and maybe I could do something to help if I'd get off my ass and try a little harder?'"

"You can't go through life like that—guilty of stuff you have nothing to do with." I take a big swig of my beer and sink my teeth into the dripping steak. I am thinking about tomorrow night and wondering how to use this moment with Quay to convince him to reconsider his plan. "Quay, I know you've thought this through, and I'm not going to tell you if what you are doing is right or wrong, but do you really want to risk doing something that you might regret your entire life?"

A crazy fire returns to his eyes, "This is off the table. Everything you have to say on this subject I've thought through a million times. What if I find out a few weeks down the road that he did this to someone else? What if someone else is permanently injured, because we did nothing? Do you think I want to live with that?"

"And the police—"

"Are useless."

That ends it. For now. But there must be some way. After we wash the dishes, Quay holds his empty beer bottle up to the light. "We have a choice Leester," he says my high school nickname, "end the night here, or go out to a bar where we can turn the night into whatever it ends up being."

As has become our custom, we start the night off with shots of tequila. I order the first round and Quay orders the second. We pull up stools and Quay defaults to talking about the work he's doing here. It's a conversation I have already heard several times, one he reverts to after his third or fourth drink.

He goes on, lost in his own words, "Well, yeah, I really like what I'm doing. But it's not my vocation. Donating my time teaching is good because education is key. You don't have a chance if you don't have an education."

To me, everything he says sounds like, "rabble, rabble, rabble."

"I think what you're doing is admirable," I say.

"What I'm doing is bullshit," he says, "Teaching kids Vanilla Ice is not doing anything. Everyone goes abroad to teach English. What's teaching English accomplishing?" Something I've never seen in him before twinkles in his eyes.

"More than I'm doing," I say.

"You really want to do something?" he finishes his Cuba Libre. A vision of the next year flashes before me. In it Stella and I are living in some third world anywhere volunteering with poor kids. Quay ruins the vision by telling me that he could help me find a charity for me to do "service work," a word that reminds me of the military, which makes me think of the camouflage my brother died in.

"I'm interested. Let's talk about it later."

"We can do it tonight."

"Do what?"

"Help people." He says help people, but his voice intonation makes it sound like he said *hurt people*.

I wave to Sara to bring us another round. She sighs and reaches for new glasses. Looking down I scan dozens of inscriptions people have carved into the wooden bar table.

Lance and Charlotte Forever!

I'm drunk.

L and D's Antigua 2012

I point one of the carvings out to Quay:

Be the Change.

He smiles, "You've been here long enough to get it. I bet you're like me and you want to really do something, yeah?"

My eyes stay focused on the table, "Everyone wants to do something."

"So let's do something then."

"Let get drunk!"

"I'm not talking about teaching. I'm talking about the Indian Jones type shit. Undercover shit. Teaching English is for English teachers. I'm not just an English teacher, Liam," he's rambled into the arbitrary rages liquor leads us. "What we should be doing, is getting people out of human trafficking."

"What we should be doing is trying out new shots," I offer, wondering if I'm slurring.

"Do you even know what human trafficking is?"

"Can't be worse than tequila, can it?"

"When I first heard it called that I thought it was like,

illegal migration. But it's slavery. You know there are more slaves in the world now than there were during the Civil War?"

"Quay, why the hell are we talking about slaves? What's wrong with you?"

"These are facts," he spits the words in my face and looks like he's going to cry," I'm not making this shit up. This isn't human smuggling. These are people taken to places against their will, forced to do things against their will. This is the lowest dirt out there. So do you want to do something or not?"

"At this particular moment, I want to drink."

"I'm being serious."

"So am I—shots my dude, shots."

"You're not even listening to me!" The liquor has him just where the liquor wants him.

"—I'm a tourist," I shout to Quay then Sarah and it feels good to yell, "We want another shot!" I turn to the crazed man seated across from me, "Quay, I have no idea what the hell you are going on about. You're like a bomb. One minute you're sitting there and then you explode and I can't keep up with what exactly you want from me right now. But if it's anything other than hanging out drinking at this bar, count me out."

"You haven't listened to me! Shut up and listen for a second. There are brothels all over, and you can bet most of the people working in them don't want to be."

"Can we talk about happy things?"

"We can actually do something real and get them out."

"What are we going to do? Break down the doors and bust out prostitutes? Where are they going to live? This is crazy talk."

He's drunk and fixated, "Screw that. I don't mean physically breaking them out. I mean we can go undercover and gather data so that we can report it."

"Report them to the police who don't do anything?" Sara is slowly counting out change to a couple at the other end of the bar, ignoring us, as bartenders do drunks whose orders they can't hear.

"No, not the police, there's another department, it's like our Justice Department, they can do something. I have a contact there."

"You have a contact there, Mr. Bond?" I say and then shout to Sara, "Can we get another drink or what!"

With a quick motion, Quay moves our empty glasses to the edge of the table. "I'm serious about this and the least you can do is hear me out."

"I'm serious too. You want another drink?"

"We can fight this shit."

"But first, a drink."

"I can't do this alone. I need a wingman."

"I'm happy to be your wingman if it means we embarrass ourselves in front of Swedish girls," I motion to a group of blonde girls sitting in the corner. "They're hot. Let's talk to them."

"You don't understand."

"Nope."

"I'll give you some articles to read. I can't do it alone—"

"—then you wouldn't be able to do it with me."

"You don't know that."

"That's apparent."

"If you understood, you'd change your mind."

"Sara, two more Cubas *por fa-frickin-vor*!"

Sara slams two Cubas down in front of us and stomps back to the other end of the bar. He's at last quiet as he sits and sips his drink with a smug look of disgust on his face. It's like he's the very idea of what he's trying to convince me has him intoxicated. Then he drops his glass back down and shakes his head, "You know what? This is why you lost all your friends. You're just a smart ass. You can't take anything seriously. Everything's a joke to you."

I cough up my drink, a sudden rage broadsiding me. "You don't have a goddamn clue what you're talking about!"

The fleshy part of his neck sags vulnerably. I look at the fork in the basket on the table, why, I don't know. Before I can yell more, Stella walks in. Not into the bar, but into my mind. And this causes my anger to turn in on itself. I see it all—how I am building up my hopes just so that they can be knocked down. I'm not the kind of guy she goes for. She's going to end up being just another thing out of my reach. I am stuck being this shitty person, in this crappy life where happiness looms, taunting always just beyond the world blabbering inside my head.

"Lost all my friends? Who the hell did you talk to? You

don't have a clue!"

"I have enough of a clue to know why all of our mutual friends don't talk to you anymore." Quay is not backing down because he must want to be forked in the neck. The bar is staring, convinced all this shouting must lead to violence. Violence has my vote. Sara behind the bar looks helpless towards us. This is what strangles me. People who have no clue what I've been through and use these little snippets of what they see to try to tell me something about me they think I don't know. "Do you know why, Quay? Do you know why? Do you know why!"

"I KNOW WHY!"

"You don't know why. You don't because it has nothing to do with your life and all you want to do is talk about yourself and why you're better than everyone else. Here's some news for you; no one cares! It's interesting maybe the first time, but give it a rest. While everyone else is making something out of their lives you're getting wasted in Guatemala teaching English to little kids and doing nothing but talk incessantly about it."

Quay pounds his fist into the table, " Judge me you asshole. Judge the shit out of me and hide from the fact that I only reached out to you and invited you here because everyone was saying that you were going to kill yourself.

"YOU DIDN'T FIND YOUR DAD DEAD QUAY!" I fire and then slam my forehead into the table to hide the tears. It's quiet here now. No talking anymore. I grab a fork from the table not because I want to hurt anyone with it, I just want to hold it. My mind flutters around like a chicken's body who's just lost his head—floundering in a flurry of post-death excitement, without a head to ask the body "What are you going to do with that fork?"

"Don't play that card with me, it's not fair. I'm on your side." Quay sets a hand on my shoulder, his voice is conciliatory. "You at least had a dad when you were a kid."

Someone at the bar is laughing.

"What are you laughing at!" My headless-chicken-body-mind makes my body stand—only then do I realize how drunk is am.

Quay gets up and leaves. Just like that, he leaves the bar. And then I sit back and nothing happens until Sara walks over and sets a drink in front of me, "If you're smart you won't drink this."

The chicken's body goes limp. It was a wild death dance but finally falls on its side. I drop the fork and it pings on the wooden floor below.

"I'm not," I say, reaching for the glass.

"Are you embarrassed?" The bartender asks.

"No," I say like a young boy.

"You're still blushing. You had it in you for a moment, but you definitely don't have it. Don't worry," she adds, "most people who have 'it' end up where they don't want to be."

"Thanks," I say.

She straightens, "I was not complimenting you. People," she grabs the empty glasses on the table, "They are all too much, you know? But they're just one of you. Just another version of the species. We're all just everyone else—"

I sit up straight and try to look composed. "I wasn't embarrassed. I was angry."

She seems about to pull away but lingers and says, "You looked like a little angry mouse." She points a finger into my chest, "Ah you see, you can still smile." Then before she walks away, says, "My parents are dead too."

I sit drinking more even though I shouldn't. How I'll get back to my bed is a tough riddle I'll solve when the time comes. The taste of whiskey on my tongue transports me to a year ago, when I tasted it before and after the phone call from my dad. A phone call to tell me that my older brother had been killed by friendly fire and I should come home. Those were the words he used, "Chris has been killed by friendly fire."

I was at the Missile Toe. It was almost midnight. Your brother, my father said to me, and he didn't even need to finish, because I could tell from his voice that I would never see Chris again.

My friends at the Missile Toe, hearing only my side of the conversation, all looked expectantly at me after I hit 'end' on my cell phone and set it on the table. Cathy hugged my shoulders and I stared down at the still glowing screen in front of me, knowing that in a few seconds those bright colors would disappear and the phone would be dark and lifeless. Half a whiskey-coke sat in front of me. I picked up the cold glass and stood before my friends. I faced them and raised my glass. They saw it in my eyes; they knew he was gone. Everyone raised their glasses without saying anything and at the time it seemed beautiful.

I never really forgave myself for how I reacted to the news of Chris's death. The next morning, in the sober daylight, I saw that the toast was for me, not him. How had I cheapened it into something so self-serving? I guess I always kinda held that against myself. The next morning he was not a fallen soldier anymore, just someone who used to be my brother. I seemed wise to avoid caring about things altogether and the future would only affirm this.

Wars, I reminded Chris the day before he left, are never between two countries, they are between two governments, and if people had the volition to stand up to their leaders and refuse to fight, there could be no war. He just smiled and asked me if I wanted anything from the desert. Then he said that if it's not worth dying for, it's certainly not worth killing for. But this was just something he picked up from one of his army buddies. There's no way he came up with it. He probably never thought about it enough to realize what a dumb-ass thing it was to say. Believe it or not, I used to care about myself and things, but then a misfired American bullet killed a soldier and the war and the world continued without seeming to notice. I wish I could care like I used to. Today, more than anything, I want to feel a certain way about certain things. Quay's an idiot, but at least he's a passionate idiot.

The bar continues to fill and my drink empties and fills again magically. I turn when I hear Sara yell, "Hey Quay! Welcome back douche. We were just talking about you. The bar voted and we decided you owe your buddy over there an apology." She pantomimes to him to move from the doorway to my table. He sits back down.

"What's she talking about?" He asks, nodding towards Sara.

"Not sure. Ask her."

"Oh."

"Yep."

Quay looks at everything but my eyes, "I'm sorry."

"You should be."

"We cool?"

"I guess."

"Friends?"

"Have we ever really been?"

"Shut up with that. Even if I'm not your first draft pick, I'm a better friend than you know."

"That doesn't actually mean anything."

"Well, whatever, I'm sorry. I just really want to do something about this human trafficking stuff. All I read are books on it. I keep saying I'll do something, but I don't ever do anything about it. I'm a lame ass, English teacher. You were right about that. It's dumb but I thought we could…I thought you and I could… you have no idea some of the stuff that goes on in the world," he gives up saying what he wanted to do.

"I think I have pretty good insights into the messed-up-edness of the world," I say as I think about the different college papers I wrote. How many college papers are being written right now? How many millions of college papers sit saved on hardrives? It's so easy to be charged and political about things in front of a computer screen, so easy to debate and debate and debate in classrooms and bars, but no one actually ever does anything. We all just fight these stupid linguistic battles that help nobody.

Quay's returned to the topic of human trafficking. "Kids forced to be prostitutes! Forced!"

I want that fire. I want to feel this strongly about anything. To care so much about something that I don't care about my own little life. Disjointed pieces of thoughts collide and fit together in an unfailing tapestry.

"Quay," I say, confident that I've found the key to a door I've been trying to break through, "how important is this to you, this human trafficking stuff?"

"Have you been listening? It's why I'm here."

"And you really think we can do something tonight?"

He jolts backward then forwards. He slides the centerpiece candle to the edge of the table so that there's nothing between us. It lights our faces with an ominous orange glow. He gauges me for sincerity and before he can speak I say four words that cause him to nearly fall off his stool, "Because I'll do it—"

"But," his face somersaults and I hold up a hypnotizing hand.

"But what?" he blurts out, holding the candle between us with both hands.

"I know I promised I wouldn't bring this up, but if you just decide to forget about this lynching thing, I'll do this with you."

"Wheels are already in motion I can't just—"

"Then let those wheels turn without you. Just bow out of it. Say you're sick; I don't care. No one is going to hold that against you.

I see gears churning in his head turning counter clockwise, trying to work out conflicting convictions. I push him further, "If you really feel as strongly about this human trafficking stuff, then show me. Because I feel as strong about you not avenging Shannon like you're planning. If you promise me you'll leave it alone, then I'll do whatever you say we should tonight."

If Quay does this, Pablo will keep his word to me, and without Pablo driving the whole thing, it will die. I imagine Stella's reaction when I tell her.

"I'm giving you a choice, Quay. I really don't want to do whatever you really want to do. I really don't want you to do that 'thing' you really do."

Quay's hand is shaking, but finally, he grabs my hand with a sweaty palm and says, "Okay."

"Okay as in, you won't do that 'thing' to the guy that sold that 'stuff' that hurt Shannon?"

"Yes, I said okay, okay? I'll stay out of it. I'll leave it up to the other guys to go through with it."

And so that settles his end of the bargain. My hands moist around my glass I ask, "So how do we do whatever you want to do?"

"The first step," Quay's glass slips from his hands and shatters on the ground. The bar crowd turns to us momentarily. An old man seated at the bar raises his hands and begins applauding wildly. Quay looks at the shards with a big smile and turns back to me, "The first step is to identify which prostitutes were trafficked and forced and which ones are there of their own free will, and when we identify them, then we report it."

"Who rescues them?"

"The investigating team rescues them."

"But who rescues them?"

"I told you, I have a contact at this government office, does this kinda stuff. It's identifying them that's the hard part.

I hear a voice behind me, "Wow those guys are drunk." I look behind me and wonder who the girl is referring to before realizing she means us.

Quay finishes up a soliloquy and I tell him, "Okay I'm in."

He shouts overjoyed. "Sara, we need two notebooks!"

Sara looks doubtfully at Quay.

"I'll pay for them, Sara. I need to order notebooks."

"They're not on the menu," she shouts back across the room.

"Liam will pay for them."

"Will he also pay for your many unpaid tabs?"

"Yes, he will."

Sara looks at me with an eyebrow raised. "Is it true?"

She rolls her eyes and skips off through the door behind her. She returns with two pocket notebooks she places in front of Quay.

"What are the notebooks for?"

"To break sex slaves out of the brothels!"

It's suddenly dawned on me that these words spoken will lead to actual events unfolding in the world.

"Quay it's late and we're drunk."

"It's the perfect cover — that's exactly who they'd expect to be visiting a brothel, drunk tourists."

"You're on another planet man?"

"It's the perfect cover," he repeated, but might think he's saying for the first time, "I can explain everything on the way, let's go."

"I think we should do some planning."

"No," he straightens, "Now or never, because I'm either in or out tomorrow."

We can't actually be about to carry this or anything out. "Two drunks who can barely stand aren't going to help anyone."

"You made me promise something I didn't want to promise. So are you in or out?"

I think about Timmy and Tommy and Bogotá. I think about Stella. I think about how exhausting it is to resist things that unfold. Something larger than my ability to understand it passes by and I want to grab it. It's there, in Quay's dilated pupils, in his desperation, his enthusiasm, his passion. He is offering me that fury. Do I want it? I see myself doing it. I see someone saved. I've already saved her. Now I'm accepting an award. I'm on Oprah, talking about my undercover work in Guatemala. L I see Stella watching, madly in love with what she sees.

> *What made you do it?*
> *Well, Oprah, the first time I was very hesitant.*
> *In a new place, a new environment.*
> *It's scary.*
> *Every time I go into these places I'm scared, but if I don't do what I do, there is no one to save them.*

Oprah: Liam, you have changed life's course for so many people caught up in tragedy.

> *I know.*
> *Thanks.*

"Fuck it. If we are going to do this, then let's do it."

Ecstatic is a good word, but not one strong enough to describe Quay's reaction. Utter elation. Why hasn't he done this before? Why does he mistakenly think he needs me? He explains with manic gestures everything I will need to know and do. We will go to a brothel and "rent" a girl. The pimp must think we are doing it for sex. "Hide your notebook and pen in your underpants and take it out when the door is shut."

Then once we're each alone with a girl, we will begin asking her questions. Well, first we will tell her that we do not want to have sex with her but instead only want to ask her some questions.

Quay assures me, "She will not tell the pimp that we didn't have sex with her for fear of a beating." The questions are simple: How old are you? How long have you been working here? What made you decide to work here? Could you leave here if you wanted to?

Quay scrawls these questions in Spanish on the first page of my notebook. "If we only ask four questions, won't we be done in a few minutes?"

"Ask them slowly. And carefully. They don't care how much time, they just want our money. Do you have cash on you? Good. We'll need at least 500Q each. I'll pay you back."

We board a Tuc-tuc and bounce over the cobblestone streets with purpose-driven force and exhilarating violence. Quay turns to me every few seconds to smile and nod. We are doing it! He says in both words and expression. He says something to the driver in Spanish. The driver looks torn, like he's on the edge of some moral precipice, but eventually nods and accelerates. "We're doing it," he says to me again, and some deep part of me looks at the scene unfolding and turns away.

CHAPTER TWENTY-ONE

Fewer and fewer people on the street marks our progress as we tumble along dark streets and alleys. Then there is no one. No cars. Just the street and us. The haphazardly spaced lights reduce in number until the only light is the tuc-tuc cab's lonely headlamp. The buildings are cinder block walls topped with barbed wire. Alone in the dim light, we stagger to a halt in front of the most depressing wall I've ever seen, concealing who knows what.

"You ready?"

No backing out now.

"Yep."

We could easily back out now. We could tell the driver to take us back to the bar and he would. No one is forcing us to go on. But some invisible energy impels us onwards. The first domino in our minds has been knocked over, and everything we do from here seems as inevitable as something already passed. Nervous excitement is in my stomach. Anticipation. Anxious dread. Adventure. Bogotá. Timmy and Tommy. A compelling life worth leading. Mine to have as a part of me. The driver grunts when we pay him, then disappears.

"How are we going to get back?"

Quay ignores me. He runs his hand over the iron door. Slowly he raises his hand and knocks. There is no answer. He knocks louder. Behind the wall I can make out the top of a building with barred windows covered with curtains. No answer.

Did the curtain just move?
Don't be so nervous.
We don't have anything to worry about.
We have so much to worry about.
I'm sure gringos go to brothels all the time.
And things go wrong all the time too.

The curtain moves again but there is too little light to see beyond the silhouette of a dark someone peering out to us. Still no answer. Quay knocks louder.

"Is it only ten?" Quay leaves this question also unanswered. "It feels later."

Then there's a knock and a voice from the other side of

the door. "*Quién es?*"

Quay puts his mouth to the door. "*Buenas noches señor. Solo nosotros. Un tuc-tuc nos trayo acá porque dice que tienen chicas las que les gustan gringos, no? Tenemos dinero para usar sus servicios amables.*"

The door is silent again. We stand in the dead street's darkness. Then the door hesitates. A mustached man with a concrete face and dirty 49ers T-shirt fills the doorway. He says nothing. He motions for us to follow. I try to escape the present. I imagine myself telling this story in a bar. That's where I want to be—safe in the future. But first, I need to get there. I put my hands in my pockets so Quay can't see the trembling. My notebook and pen are there. The wall was hiding nothing—dirt with a stone path leading to the two-story building behind. Car parts litter the dirt. The house behind the wall is dark. Music that sounds like the theme song of a children's show is coming from behind the inner door. We've made it this far, so that means this is really happening.

We walk into the building. A single bulb hangs from the center of the vacant room. Concrete. Everything is concrete. We are drunk, but learning to master the moment of this decision. It smells like the basement of a U.S. home built before the '50s. The man motions for us to wait in the entry room and disappears behind a curtain leading away. There are no windows. Quay takes a deep breath and smiles at me. His smile says, this is it—showtime.

At times my nervousness becomes a sort of serenity. This is Zen. We are here. Things are in motion. Whatever is going to happen is going to happen. It's too late to change this. Even if we have already failed, whatever. We are here to deal with whatever consequences of that.

The man comes back and addresses Quay, "Cuatro."

"Cuatro?"

"Cuatro!"

"He wants four hundred from each of us."

I reach into my pocket and feel not enough. "What if I don't have it?."

Prices are fixed Liam! This-isn't-the-place-for-this-conversation!"

"I only have seven hundred and some change."

He turns back to the man. "*Solo tenemos siete y pico? Está bien?"*

The man's expression is tired. Like he would be disgusted if he were not so exhausted with dealing with people and their never-ending stream of frustrations. His rolling eyes indicate that this is not bien, but whatever. He takes the money from me and crumples it into his pocket. I touch my notebook and remember that we are here to bring this man down. To bring him to justice. I remember that there are people here who we do not hate, people lost we have come to find.

He motions and we follow him behind a curtain. There is a hallway that leads through a room where two other gruff Guatemalan men are seated in front of cards on a rusted table situated above a pile of garbage. They don't look at us. They glare at their hands. These are bad men, I remind myself. Up a dingy staircase is another hallway. The further we go the dirtier everything becomes. Scratches in the grime are the only indication of the underlying concrete. There are a half dozen doors, two are open. He motions us to the doors, "*Tienen media hora.*"

"He says we have half an hour."

I walk into one of the rooms and close the door behind me and there she is. A nearly-naked young woman is sitting on the bed. She is wearing a black blouse reaching her upper thigh. In all of the possibilities, I never actually considered that she would be an actual person. There is a real girl in this room with me. I glance around and see the grime of this place has streaked with darkness, the single bulb swaying above us.

And here I am. And there she is. And here we are. The girl just sits on the bed waiting for me to do something. I stand in front of the door, stupid, drunk, an fool of idiotic proportions to have come here. When I remember why I am here, I flash out my notebook. I can't read any of the unintelligible letters Quay scribbled for me to ask her. There is no way she speaks English. The girl takes off her blouse with one quick motion and is all of a sudden naked.

How am I supposed to ask these questions if she is naked?
What the hell-on-earth am I doing here?

The nude girl on the bed motions for me to approach her. She is a person. I am a person. We are people. I take a single step towards the bed. My heartbeat migrates to my head. To my ears. I can't even remember the words I am supposed to ask her in English—much less Spanish. I don't want to be here. I want to run for it, but there's nowhere to run. This must be what people about to lose consciousness feel. I shuffle until I am standing at the foot of the bed.

Idiotically, I hover over the bed. She moves near me and places her hands behind my calves, slowly moving her fingertips across my jeans. I hold my notebook up to my face and ask, "*Tú Bien?*" while pointing to the floor—my feeble attempt at asking if she is here of her own will.

"*Sí, bien*," her voice is jagged.

She grabs my hand and pulls me so that I am sitting on the bed next to her. Her deeply haunting eyes are still gentle, still motherly, in spite of it all.

Why is she here?
Does she want to be here?

Her eyes seem to hold answers to everything the divide between our languages prevents us from knowing.

How old could she be?
"*Cuántos años?*"

She says nothing. She is so small, even for a Guatemalan. A Mayan. She could be twenty or fifteen. No she couldn't be fifteen. Her eyes view the world like she's seeing it for the first time. She tries to kiss my neck and I push her away so that she is sitting beside me.

A long sigh says, so nothing is ever made easy for me?

We sit staring. Neither expected our lives to be in the same room. She waits, searching for some cue. Her breasts are small and humble. They seem innocent and harmless. They're an illusion. She looks curiously at my notebook to avoid my eyes and then moves her gaze haphazardly about the room. There is nothing in the room to see but bare bleakness—the moldy mattress defining the singular purpose of the space. I look at the curtained and barred window and realize it must have been her peering at us from the street. I have never seen an emptier room. My head has filled with lead.

Either a minute or fifty have passed. I turn the page of my notebook. It's white and empty. She sighs again, you are torturing me. Do what you came to do, but do not make me wait. The anticipation is what kills me too.

"*Cómo te, Cómo te llamas,*" I manage. For the first time we look at each other. She looks searchingly into my eyes, *what is my name to you?*

There is something crudely primordial about those eyes, speaking the language before languages.

What is my name to you?

She is naked ten thousand years ago. When men and women lived in trees and caves, and only in rare instances came across outsiders. How a man would see a woman unknown to him, both naked, passing in the woods. How they would have no common language but would look at each other with a garnering gaze. Who was friendly? Who was savage? How they would feel love or lust or fear. How it used to be the same thing. If the woman or man ran away or if one chased the other. Or if they just stood gazing, acknowledging each other's existence before parting forever into separate worlds.

She points to my crotch and nods insecurely, let me do what I have to do. Let be done what you came here to do.

She sits close to me. She smells like Walmart shampoo. Her little fingers reach for the top button of my fly. I move her hand away. I am drunk. I want to run away.

I drift so very far away from myself until I am just an observer of an overly fucked up world. A six-year-old Liam peers from the furthest corner of my mind. The Liam who held his mom's hand, and in the other held a plastic bag filled with pine cones, feathers, leaves, whatever I saw as precious on the forest floor. Whose dad asked him what he found, who released his mother's grip to show him all of the pine cones and feathers. Whose father said, "Wow," impressed by these finds. Whose father went into the garage because he wanted to die.

The inevitable absence, the passing of time, the inescapability of change, and that boy, somehow led to this adult, led to me, next to a naked prostitute, maybe a slave, possibly a child and that six-year-old boy's future is wondering how collecting pine cones and leaves led to this. Who then recoiled, alarmed that an unimaginable debate going on inside.

A drunk mind still knows a dark path when it sees one. But who is anyone to judge this situation from the outside? Who is anyone to know what it is like to be inside someone else's head? What responsibility do I have to this girl? Her life sucks and I hate it. But if not me, then who will help her? And if me, how? I want to give her all the money I have, but I have nothing left.

Six year old Liam, who, after showing the contents of the bag to his dad, set down the bag, and holding his mother's hand with his left and his father's with his right, was lifted in the air as they chanted One, two, three up! And then they would lift my small body into the air. I can see Grandma's house, I told them. And though it was hundreds of miles away, I swear I could.

She touches my jeans, and her hands are gentle and slow. I could save her. I could take her away from here. *You can't even save yourself, Liam.*

She reaches for my zipper, but I wave her to stay away. I look sorrowfully at the confused face of a girl. She closes her eyes. I fill the blank pages in front of me with these words:

Dear Mom,

She puts her face in her hands.
The world can shatter faith in anything.
She begins to sob.

I write:

Mom, I love you in spite of anything and am sorry for being distant.
We can't fix the broken things,
but we can make new things.

She stops crying as abruptly as she began. She looks up at me, a strange new kind of human who came here to write besides her. Alcohol is in charge of my body—which only knows how to crave. My mind knows nothing. My body is here, but where am I? Am I here somewhere too? What does my mind know? Something surreal passes soberly in front of me. On the verge of two lives. She reaches towards me but again I wave her hand away.

I see myself sitting on a bed. Not this one. Some future bed. With my head in my hand, hating this moment, hating myself more. The vision is clearer than what's immediately in front of me. I see my past and future in vivid completeness, and then we both jump together. Just beyond the door is horrible shouting. Several people.

Is that Quay's voice?

She jumps to the other side of the bed and looks down, crossing her legs and arms to cover her thin body.

BOOM!
A gunshot.
A GUNSHOT!
A gunshot?
A gunshot.
Holyshitagunshot.

The window has bars on it. There is only the door behind which is a chorus of angry Spanish. Rapid, machine gun Spanish is rising in volume. Who could a gun have shot? I listen for Quay's voice, but it is not there. I cannot stay. But there are bars on the window. Only one decision lies trembling, unmastered in front of me.

WhatdoIdowhenthereisnothingtodo?
Where's Quay's voice?
Quay is dead.
You don't know that.

I know Quay is dead. He is dead or going to die. This is what we deserve for being morons. There's been a gunshot. *Who will ever know I was not here for the worst reasons imaginable?* We should have left a letter with someone explaining this all. I should have done so many other things.

The decision is made for me. The Guatemalan who answered the door throws open the door to the room that somehow was not even locked.

Why didn't I lock the door when I came in?
It~doesn't~matter!

He grabs me by the arm and drags me out to the hall. Quay is shaking uncontrollably with his back against the wall and two Guatemalans are standing in front of him with guns in their malicious hands. He has no shirt. Where the hell is his shirt? I am dragged next to him. The Guatemalans have his notebook and do not look happy.

"Who~got~shot?"
"No~one~got~shot!"
"There~was~a~shot."
"No~one~got~shot!"

"Shut the fuck up!" I am surprised that the Guatemalan in front of me speaks English. "No English."

This excludes me from speaking.

They question Quay in Spanish, but he can't seem to understand them.

What the hell is he going to do with pepper spray?

Quay has produced a can of pepper spray and is holding it in trembling hands like a moron.

What the hell does he think he is going to do with pepper spray?
Why is his shirt off?

One of the men slaps his pitiful canister to the ground and laughs.

"What~are~they~saying?"

"I say no fucking English!"

This will end when someone dies. Someone will die, I am sure. I am going to die. Quay is going to die. We are going to die. My mom will find out that I was killed in a brothel. Or worse, will never hear from me.

Will she think I left her too?
Who would ever suspect the truth?

No one ever knows or understands anything ever.

They have his notebook. They are not happy with what has been written.

They point to it and then him, "Qué es esta mierda?" We are drunk. They seem drunk. They don't know what to do either. Quay's knees crash into each other.

"What~did~you~do?" I ask without turning to him.

A man takes his pistol and bangs it into the concrete wall, "No fucking English!"

Three of them, angry. And two of us, scared. We the idiotic boys, playing kid's games with men. Both sides are trapped for opposite reasons. I feel I'm losing life already. Maybe I'll faint before I die. This would be preferable. And that is the worst this situation has to offer. Death seems too trivial to be the worst case scenario.

You see the death of yourself and your friends in slow motion. You see the man pull the trigger. You see Quay's chest erupting with little volcanoes of blood. He moans on cue, has one more decisive look, like remembering where he put his keys, and then you see him fall to the ground. Then the man points the gun at you and pulls the trigger. Only when you don't die do you realize this only happens in your mind. Quay is terrified like me but is alive.

The gun changes time like a magic wand. Every thought follows its direction. I run back into the room. I lock the door. The girl is not screaming. Just standing naked, still. I lock the door. A pound pounds the door. Pounds, pounds, slamming into the metal of her prison. The locked door is still the only way out. Cinderblock walls and one window with big, fat metal bars I hate.

The pound still pounds. The girl is not covering up. Just standing there, naked. The pound is the sound of the butt of a gun against metal. Threats in a language that means nothing to me.

No hope here. These bars are meant to keep someone inside. The men with the guns outside. There's no way out. The booze in my head. The girl by my side. The horrible feeling. The motion of time. The way your heart knows the only way to find stillness is to accept the inevitability of it all. The way this feeling first feels like defeat, but then like liberation because finally you know: this is it. The only way to meet death is humbly, dumbly. To go like a lamb who's always known her destiny was a slaughterhouse.

The girl unlocks the door. The soft dream of death is awakened by the nightmare of life. The men storm in. They grab me and pull me and punch me in the stomach. The girl stands frozen with her hand in the air parallel to the door's lock —Pandora, astounded at the contents of her box. I can't breathe.

A new man is outside. There are four men. The new man asks in a deep voice "what the feck have you lads done?" He is bearded and turns to me in English, "It's you again, eh?" He looks at the three angry Guatemalans cornering us with guns. "Shite, what the feck did you guys feckin' do, kill a feckin' prostitute?"

He speaks to the bad men in machine-gun Spanish and they point to us in accusing gestures. They are so angry. They show him the notebook. I catch my breath and recognize him. The bearded man. The drunken Irish man who wanted $25 from me at the bar when I first arrived. He takes the notebook and points to me. "What the hell are you doing writing this shite? Don't you feckin' know better? What the feck kind place do you think this feckin' is?" I can't imagine he could recognize me after the black-out wasted state he met me in.

They go back and forth again in Spanish. The bearded man and Joes looks from them to us and shakes his head at me. This frustration is not murder. This frustration is children. Children sneaking cookies again. They are aggravated but see we are so clearly harmless. Drunk gringos. So clearly scared. So clearly incapable. They would have already killed us. In the movies it happens bam, bam. What happened to Quay's shirt?

Joes turns to me and says, "Okay feck bags. You need to get the feck out of here right feckin' now or you are both going to be thrown in a feckin' garbage bag and dumped in a feckin' ditch. You're feckin' lucky they respect me and I don't know why I should feckin' waste my respect on you. So feckin' pay them a hundred dollars now and get the feck out of here."

"We don't have any money."

"Well then they are going to kill you...feck I am just kidding. Don't soil your feckin' knickers. But this is shite, you can't pull shite like that with these guys."

I remember that I still don't know what we've done. There is some conversation. The Guatemalans don't seem completely pacified by whatever Joes is saying.

"Okay, give me your feckin' wallets."

The Guatemalans search us, emptying our pockets. They take the notebook from mine and look at the words I've written in English. They show this to Joes. He translates it for them. This seems to calm them a bit. One laughs. He says something and Joes translates, "He says you are a gay."

They take my wallet, which is empty, except for an ATM card and a movie rental card for a store that closed a decade ago. They strike me as Netflix people anyways.

"Okay, now get the feck' out of here now. You guys really know how to piss dangerous people off. Shite man, these guys are nice blokes until you pull shite with them." Joes is addressing me, the whole time ignoring Quay, who is obviously the reason these guys are so pissed off.

We are taken to the door and shoved out into the street.

"Holy shit," Quay exhales, looking out at the dark and empty road.

"Holy shit?" I repeat as a question.

"Holy fucking shit," he says again with a smile, still shirtless.

And that's when I look at Quay and feel something

break in me. Or rather, break through me.

"You asshole piece of shit!" I clench my fists and watch as Quay's smile falls to the gravel road and I say, "You dumb shit idiot, what the fucking hell did you think was going to happen! It's by sheer dumb stupid luck that we are even alive."

And even though I'm drunk off liquor and rage I know that I am the dumb one, I am the one foolish enough to have followed a fool. And so I know that this is not about him. I shout the most vicious words I know. Things no human should say to another. But really, I'm shouting at God, at the President for going to war, at my brother for joining that war, and at every shattered thing littering the world. I shout until pain cuts off my voice and run before Quay or anyone in the world sees the shattered tears coming to take over where anger leaves off.

CHAPTER TWENTY-TWO

I wish I knew a guy with a shrunken head collection.
"*Why?*" I hope she'll say.
Because I bet a guy like that would be hella interesting to know, I'll say.

Even if she doesn't jump in with the, "*Why?*" it's fine. After a pause, I'll plow right through to the punch line. This is the latest in a dozen of potential opening lines I've shaped for my date with Stella. I like this one because it's intelligent, ethnic —the shrunken head part is—and it's the kinda stupid humor I think she goes for. And if she starts off laughing, what more can I want?

I'm early, alone at the calm before this bar's storm. It gives me more time to rehearse other conversational scenarios —what she might say, what I'll say back if she does. I had to fight just to get here. The streets outside are bleeding people. People can't seem to get enough of Holy Saturday.

How much small talk do I need before telling her about the other night's success? It's not 100%. It only means that Pablo and Quay are out, but with the only Guatemalan dropping out, I don't think a bunch of scared-to-death gringos are going to lynch a guy on their own. I will probably say "lynch" with finger quotation marks when I tell Stella. But maybe not; some people find that annoying. Better not try anything too crazy too early on.

In a best-case scenario, I tell her about how I got Pablo and Quay to opt-out and she'll play success's advocate and be the one to convince me that she is completely sure they won't go through with the plan. Then I'll casually brush it off and say something like, " I did what anyone else would have done in the same situation."

But no matter how many variations of combinations I live out in my head, the conversation that takes place will be completely different from anything I thought it would be. Only other people can do that, break us out of the lowest denominator that we become when we're not working to fit someone else's unpredictability in our life.

The weathered, surfer-looking dude behind the bar doesn't seem to have plans to attend my table, so I raise my hand when his eyes pan over mine and say over the afternoon drone that I'd like a Cuba Libre.

He hops off the waist-high beer cooler he's sitting on and says, "I don't do table service, bro."

"That's cool with me," I stand up and walk to the bar.

"Yeah, because sometimes people complain about that, and when they do, I just look them square in the eyes and I just tell them. 'I. Just. Don't. Do. Table. Service. Bro.'"

"Roger that," I tell him, exchanging money for change and cradling my drink back to the table.

I interrogate the clock with a glare, but the more I pay attention to it, the slower it moves. 40 minutes before our official rendezvous time. She could be early. She also could be here on Guatemalan time: late. I drink my Cuba slowly. 39 minutes till go time.

It might be better if I showed up and she was waiting for me. That's the way to go. The best thing would be to arrive exactly at seven, or a few minutes after so that she doesn't think that I am as eager about seeing her as I am. Gotta play it cool. I'll leave, walk around outside to come back in a half an hour or so.

All week the Holy week crowds and impromptu processions have been crescendoing. Despite the struggle to get through the people to get in the bar, I'm fighting even more to get out. There's no flow of people, everyone is just standing in the streets, and to get from one block to another requires squeezing through hundreds of people one must push out of the way.

It's gotten dark in the short time I spent inside. I squeeze through past two Mayan women with children tied to the backs of their dresses. Kids who couldn't be older than twelve are carrying toddlers in proud arms. Venders rush by selling noisemakers and styrofoam lizards on wire leashes. The cobblestone streets are lined with clusters of people meticulously laying down flowers, plants, pine needles, and colored sawdust.

I tap a gringo taking pictures with a camera large enough to be a rifle, "What's going on?"

"The devil's procession's going to come through here soon. It's gonna be insane."

Before he can say more, we're both separated by the crowd. I push my way to the edge of the street and look at carpets being created. The streets are slowly being clothed from the assorted piles of brightly colored sawdust and pine needles heaped about every few feet in the center of the street.

Carpets for procession, beautiful patterns. People all around, music. It's no wonder the bar was nearly empty. Who would want to hang out in a tavern when everything worthwhile is happening outside? I push my way around the corner to La Merced church where a million vendors are selling food and candy and toys and confetti and a wide assortment of who-knows-what. Below my waist children have staked their claim at the corners beneath the vending tables where they are conducting themselves by their own rules in the worlds of their own makings.

"*Cuánto?*" I ask a woman sweating behind a cotton candy machine.

"*Diez,*" she tells me, already reaching for a paper cone to swirl the rotating sugar below into a pink club of deliciousness.

The cotton candy sticks to any part of my body it can and soon my lips and the unshaved beginnings of a beard are covered in a hot mess that is not cool just before a date. I order a bottle of water and wash myself over the fountain. A half-dozen couples are seated on the stone rim of the fountain intently lost in each other's lips. I wash over the fountain and then begin to break through the crowd and push my way back to the bar, tripping over more people than I would have ever guessed could fit into one street or world.

I take a place at the table I had occupied before. Outside a few tourists bellied up to the bar, it's still a quiet escape from the pandemonium overflowing in the streets. 7:03 and she's not here.

The clock reluctantly progresses till 7:05 and at 7:07 I walk up to the bar and order another Cuba libre. She walks in at 7:11 and I make a wish and take a long cool drink before standing up.

"Hey," I kiss her cheek and go in for a hug, but she pulls away and sits down at the table. Damn, I was going to pull her chair out for her.

"Wanna grab a drink here first?" I suggest.

"Where?"

"Here."

"Were you waiting for a while? It's impossible outside with all those people."

"No, not long. I was checking out all the craziness going on outside."

"Yeah, they should rename Holy Week, 'can't get anywhere' week. I was planning on skipping town by now, it's too crazy."

"I was thinking though while I was waiting, it would be really, really cool to know a guy who had a shrunken head collection."

"What the hell does that have to do with anything we were talking about?"

"What were we talking about?"

"Not shrunken head collections.'

"Guess what."

"What?" She turns away from me to peer out the barred window.

"I got Quay and Pablo not to do it."

"Do what?"

"The 'lynching thing.'" I make air quotes that I instantly regret.

"What? Why the hell would you do that?"

"You wanted me to do that?"

"What are you talking about? When did I tell you I wanted you to do that?"

"When I first met you. Well I mean, the second time I saw you, you said something like 'curing pain with more pain is dumb.' And before that you said the same thing. That's the first thing we ever talked about."

Her eyes roll back to me, "Who the fuck are you to screw around with everyone else's business?"

"I don't mean I did it for you. I did it because it was the right thing to do."

"So now some psychopath, who almost killed Shannon, is going to be on the loose because you stopped the only people that were going to stop him? Wow, thanks for being here a couple weeks and getting involved in stuff you don't know anything about."

"Hold on. So if I convince them to get back on board with murder is that going to be a good thing to do? Or are you going to change your stance on this again?"

She says nothing. Just shakes her head at me.

"I kept thinking that your hard exterior is hiding someone I want to know, but more and more it seems like this is it."

"I got an idea," she claps her hands together and twists a smile on her face, "Let's change our plans and go to a brothel tonight. That sounds way better than stir-fry, sí?"

Quay and I swore not to tell anyone. "What's up with you?"

"Nothing. I just thought it sounds like fun. Doesn't it sound like fun?"

Music from an approaching marching band sounds in the distance. Stella's face is filled with artificial elevation. I finish my drink as decisively as I can.

"If this is about where I was on Thursday, if for some reason someone thought this should be public business, you should know that I wasn't there for why people go there, so let me explain."

"I don't know what you are talking about. Don't you think it would be fun to go to a brothel, get a few prostitutes?

"We were there to try to find a way to help the women forced to work there. We were there to do a good thing."

"Well, you wouldn't want to do a bad thing poorly."

"If I hadn't gone there, they'd still be plotting to... to do that thing. Do you want to know the truth or do you want to be unfair like everything else in this world?"

"..."

"Can I explain?"

"Explain what?"

"Really?"

"No, I mean, I don't care."

"Who told you..." two disjointed dots connect. "Joes... your friend Joes."

"I said it doesn't bother me."

"Well your body language makes a good case for it."

"Do you speak Body Language better than you speak Spanish?"

"If you're not mad, then you're mean."

"What's my body language saying to you now?" she gyrates and cups her hands around her breasts.

"Whatever Joes told you, he doesn't know. He doesn't know why we were there. I was with Quay, and we were there to–." My words break apart and I don't bother to pick up the pieces. Stella holds up a halting hand and excuses herself to go to the bathroom, but I watch her walk out the door.

Do I run after her? The bartender gives me a nod, "Girls bro, they're all scallawags."

Beyond the threshold of the bar is the apocalypse. Chaos bounces off itself. Everyone is smashing me into the bar's stucco walls. The crowd squints through the incense smoke and kids take to their parent's shoulders. The odds of me finding her in this unyielding mass of people is nil. But she's in this crowd somewhere. She must be. All of Antigua is here. I push through everyone in my way. They sway like stubborn branches. Under their glares, I make my way from one congested area to another.

It's like a parade on acid. In front of me a pregnant woman is holding the two small hands of her children. To her left a blind man is hitting everyone with his cane. Young, embarrassed women line the walls, deliberating casting their eye contact. Dogs occupy a world below everyone's waist as they run from one happy errand to the next.

People from everywhere. Pigeons everywhere. People carrying fires in metals bowls at the end of chains fill the evening with their smoke. There are jugglers and dancers, drunks, and popcorn venders, people playing guitar, and people walking with their dogs and families. There are kids strapped to kids carrying younger kids and old Mayan women shuffling along in slow packs and a woman selling mangoes with a vengeance.

They are all moving because behind them the procession is coming. The music is bleak and growing. Men carrying medieval banners mark the beginning of the procession. These are not the Purple People. The purple robes have been replaced with black robes. Emerging from the smoke is a 30-foot platform supporting a cross holding Jesus' corpse.

The carpets adorning the streets that were put together all day are being shredded by thousands of feet. Black everywhere. Black robes to hide everyone in a solemn darkness Men carrying torches and drums, drums, drums. Police dressed all in black, patrol the fringes. Jesus' corpse disappears into the smoke as the music reaches a storming volume. A dark float carrying a skeleton with a red glowing scythe matching his glowing eyes moves by, followed by a statue of Mary with her head bowed in prayer. Stella is nowhere to be found. She's been swallowed by everything else.

CHAPTER TWENTY-THREE

My hostel is filled to capacity and everyone is here to temporarily escape the relentless fiesta exploding in the streets. A glance reveals mostly fresh faces. Two blonde girls have just arrived, carrying hefty backpacks filled with their temporary lives.

I begin slowly putting the mound of stuff on my bed back into my suitcase. A barefooted Australian asks me if I know a good tour company to climb the volcano. I refer him to the agency across the street. I tell him I doubt there'll be any tours until after Easter and he thanks me and exits aimlessly.

I didn't do anything wrong, I tell myself again. I just wanted things to be like I imagined they could be. But they never are. The only thing I did wrong, and always do wrong, is delude myself into believing that things get better. If it wasn't the brothel, it would have been something else that took her away. She's someone who needs to be broken, and you can't get close to someone like that without coming apart. I should know.

I throw my accumulated garbage of paper, flyers, wrappers, and empty bottles into the plastic wastebasket by my bed and move on to the next items—dirty laundry, a flashlight I never used, a first aid kit, the camera I never used. When everything is back in my suitcase, I pick up the three books on the Maya I borrowed from the book exchange and put them back on the shelf.

A tanned brunette is perusing the shelf as I replace them. She picks up one of the books and smiles at me, "Any good?"

I pause to consider if they are. "Well, I read it with a raging fever, so I probably experienced them differently than most, but I liked it. It's sort of sad. It makes you wonder a lot about how the past could have been different, and since the past is what it was, it eats at you a little bit."

She mulls this over. "Well, it's gotta be better than all the romance novels they have here."

Our eyes move from the cover of the book to the shelf.

"I guess it depends on what you're into," my smile is sincere and I hope for her happiness in a way I wish I could for myself.

"Have you been here a while?"

"Yeah, a little over two weeks. But it feels much longer."

"How much longer are you staying then?"

"I'm on my way out. It's been war out there in the streets with Holy Week. If I can survive today, I'll make it out alive. I just booked a plane ticket home a few hours ago. I leave tomorrow."

"Ah, too bad." She seems genuinely disappointed by my pronto departure.

"So it is. What direction are you going?"

"South. I just came from Mexico."

"Well, enjoy the book."

"Thanks, happy travels."

It's Easter and the weather has changed. Dark clouds have silently overtaken the clear skies. People are talking about rain. Gray Guatemalan men are huddled in somber circles pointing up and nodding in agreement about something.

"I thought the rainy season doesn't start until May," I offer to the English guy at our hostel who seems to talk incessantly about the weather.

"Well, the weather's been weird lately. Last rainy season it hardly rained at all and then it rained every day for the first month of the dry season. So who knows?"

"It's just rain though," I say, hoping it's something more.

My companion lets out a measured sigh. "If you've experienced a tropical downpour on full blast, you don't say things like that."

CHAPTER TWENTY-FOUR

I look up at the dark clouds and hope it pours down before my plane takes me away. I hope the streets turn to rivers from relentless meteorology and every bit of Holy Week dust is taken to far away riverbeds to be finally dumped in the sea.

In 22 hours a shuttle will pick me up from my hostel and take me to the airport which will lead me to a plane, to take me back to everything.

Who will I be then?

I'm walking to Quay's apartment, so it must be to say goodbye. I haven't seen him since Friday and I don't really want to see him or know what I'll say. I'd be making a point if I just left and he didn't hear anything more from me. But I need to ask him WTF. What the hell set those guys off and what was he thinking? Whatever it was, it was seriously his fault.

But first I have a rendezvous with Pablo. I'm holding my ground on the designated corner and he materializes 30 minutes late. A beat-up guitar is slung over his shoulder.

"You play guitar, that's right." I say, remembering his invitation I declined.

"Yes, for many years. It helps me to feel okay when I don't," he runs his hand over the chipped wood.

"I wish I could have heard you play."

"I would play now, but the people and noise is too great." He grabs my arm when the crowd tries to separate us, "I keep my promise to you."

"I knew you would," I tell him, wondering how Quay told him how things came about. "I hope that's the right thing."

"Maybe the guy becomes a good person after this?"

"Maybe," I pull out a notebook and ask him to write his contact so that we can stay in touch. After a half-hug, we disappear in different directions into the crowd.

Next Quay's door looms in front of me. With so much still going on in the streets, I wonder if he's home. I didn't call him or anything. I need to knock. What is there to say? He brought me here to Guatemala. I owe him at least that. But something brought him here, and who knows if we're better or worse as a result?

My fist bangs out a rhythm on his metal door and I call his name. A fading scent of marijuana escapes with the opening door.

"Hey," he says without inviting me inside, "I was just about to go get some street food in the park, you wanna come?"

He gives me an awkward hug in the entryway and I tell him that I was just coming to say goodbye, that I'm leaving tomorrow.

"Leaving already? That's horrible. I thought you were going to stay way longer. A month is so little time and you haven't even seen the rest of the country yet."

"Two weeks."

"Yeah, two weeks. Even worse."

Quay lives far enough from the center of town that for most of the walk we don't have to fight through hordes of people. We walk mostly in silence, only interrupted by musing about the dark clouds and what it's like in the rainy season. This is a conversation of old men who have already seen everything and over-discussed it to the point where impending weather is all there is left to chat about.

"The rains only last like an hour or two," he says. "Some people are under the impression that it rains all day every day in the rainy season, but it's really not that bad. It's usually just a few hours of rain."

"I hope I get to see some of that before I leave."

"Anything's possible, those clouds don't look like they're playing around."

We stop in front of tables along the church of Central Park where Mayan women are attending to different meats sizzling on homemade grills. We opt for sausage sandwiches covered in a thick layer of avocados and spicy chili. Quay's white shirt turns out a poor choice and fills with green and red blotches. He looks from his shirt to me to see if I notice and shakes his head, "I'm like a five-year-old kid."

"And I forgot to bring moist towelettes."

"I don't understand how so many people, people like you, can eat food like this and not get it all over."

"We don't enjoy it as much as you do," I offer.

He nods. Anxiety hangs between us. Neither will mention Friday. I want to hear myself tell him that he should have listened to me, that we should have never gone to a brothel sloshed out of our minds. I want to hear him agree with me, and see him shake his head while looking at the ground and hear him tell me that I was right.

"So," I say, wishing I was braver, "this is it then."

He seems expectant, waiting for me to say the words I wish I would say. But then, inexplicably; I don't care. It doesn't matter—it won't fix or break or build or destroy or change anything. Telling Quay what he already knows does nothing for me or him. I am alive, things happened as they did, and whatever the hell Quay did, he did it to himself and who am I to pretend I wasn't a willing party to every bit of it? When we make eye contact it is mutually uncomfortable. He takes my extended hand and I put my hand on his shoulder.

"Thank you," I tell him.

"It was my pleasure. It was great seeing you down here. Sorry for— Well, you caught me at a strange time in my life, you know?"

"I mean it," I keep my hand on his shoulder, "Thank you, Quay. I'm glad I came here. I wouldn't have if it wasn't for you. It didn't matter where I went, but I can see now how much I needed to go."

Our handshake turns into the "guy" hug that is a combination of a handshake and a normal hug. He seems more relaxed afterward, both of us saying or hearing what we needed to. He seems about to walk away, but doesn't. "Are you going to see Stella before you leave?"

"What do you know about that?"

"Nothing, just that," he pauses and assesses me, " It's pretty clear you had a thing for her."

"No, I'm not going to see her, things went the wrong way."

"You have nothing to lose. Not like you're ever going to see her after Monday." Then Quay shrugs and shakes my hand and taps my shoulder, "It's good you came." I watch as he walks away to who-knows-where, to do who-knows-what, and I notice that the temperature has dropped and wonder if, when, and how I'll ever see him again.

In front of me are the ubiquitous park pigeons invisible to everyone else. Beyond them several mangy dogs look lost in the rich scents of meat sizzling a few feet beyond them—a delicious impossibility that will never be theirs. Unless of course some gringo with time to kill and Quetzales to burn steps into their lives and says, "Dogs, you have been chosen to take part in the first annual Holy Easter Feeding of the Street Dogs."

I reach into my pocket and point to a piece of meat inquiringly.

"*Quince quetzals*," the Mayan woman says looking at the wad of crumpled bills in my hand. I pull out a dirty 50Q note and push it towards the woman while holding up three fingers.

"*Trés*," I tell her, looking at the dogs who have no idea what is about to go down.

She pulls out a paper plate and starts filling it with tortillas and vegetables from plastic containers. I want to tell her that I just want the meat and don't need these sides. But with my few dozen words of Spanish vocabulary, any attempt would spiral into her not knowing what I want and me getting the tortillas and vegetables anyways.

She hands me the overflowing plate. Four dogs watch the paper plate as I shuffle it from one hand to the other. They are hoping for accidents, for my failure to hold onto anything. They know nothing of my intentions, only of the constancy of how reality has always been to them.

You're not just leaving here.
You're going back there.
Hush.

I wait and the woman hands me my change. She gives me five coins that I put in my pocket to save for the next beggar. I take the mass of tortillas and throw it towards the mass of pigeons by the fountain. The dogs look from what I've thrown to what remains on my plate.

I take two steps towards them. The one closest to me backs up, fearing a kick or some other unexpected violence my species shows his. I pick up a slab of carne asada steak and dangle it in the air. They all share the same no-way-in-hell-he-is-about-to-do-what-I-think-he-might-maybe-perhaps-be-about-to-do look. I throw the first chunk to the dogs. They jump to their feet. Three run away. They are used to rocks. The boldest creeps up to the fallen meat, sniffs the air about it, and then lunges towards the steak. When the other three see this is not some sadistic human scam, they run towards the other dog trying to get at the steak he has already consumed. I throw two more pieces of meat towards them. The one who ate the first one lunges for the largest piece, while a limping gray dog, vaguely resembling a lab, pounces on the second. A third dog, a female, with teats sagging to the ground, just watches, longing to have been brave enough to taste the steak.

I throw all that remains and the dogs vacuum it up until it's gone. The woman behind the grill points to her grill full of meat encouragingly, I laugh and tell her "es todo."

When they see I have nothing more to give, the dogs circle and lie down near their previous spots, next to where the grilling is happening, and meat returns to being something just out of their reach.

I have nothing left to do in Guatemala except wait. Clouds threaten, but rains don't come. I plant on a park bench to watch the people passing by but am soon joined by someone with untrustworthy eyes. He sits down at the other edge of the bench, slowly inching his way towards me, smiling to himself, watching me, he thinks nonchalantly, out of the corner of his eyes.

He must be about sixteen, in ragged jeans, with a few noticeable scars that have aged into his young face. His eyes are taking in everything happening around him, but doesn't realize that I am watching him as carefully as he is studying me. He inches his way next to me and says under his breath,

"Yo what you want, man? You want some weed? cocaine?"

"I would like 8 pounds of marijuana."

"Yes?"

"I want 20 pounds of cocaine."

"Come on man, what you want?' he looks hurt.

"I want nothing," and I truly mean it.

He nods, sensing I'm a dead-end and inches his way back to the other end of the bench before sauntering off. He doesn't know he's still being watched. He stands in one part of the park and then moves to another. When he sees two gringos walking up he drifts carefully over to them and they shake their heads to whatever he says and he shuffles away.

He seems aimless, but there's careful intentionality behind his movements. I see him noticing an old woman in a blue dress leaning against a tree for support. She looks exhausted from the madness of Holy Week. The boy circles her and reaches a hand into his jacket. He watches his perimeter and before anyone has any idea what is happening, she is screaming and no longer has her purse. He runs away with it under his jacket. His right hand has a knife he is trying unsuccessfully to shove back into his jacket pocket, while holding the purse in his left hand and running as fast as he can away from the woman, who is drawing attention away from the fleeing thief by upsetting the crowd with her panicked screams.

    I don't know what I am doing until my legs are already doing it. I tumble from the bench and trip into a sprint aimed for the armed mugger, who's getting away with the elderly woman's purse. My long, white, hairy gringo legs are twice as long as the assailant's legs. I catch up to him towards the edge of the park, but have no idea what to do now, so we are running beside each other—like we're out for a friendly jog. He no longer is trying to put his knife in his pocket but flashes it threateningly in front of my face, baring his teeth like a dog.

    Maybe on purpose, but probably on accident, my left gringo leg sidesteps the Boy With The Knife's little right leg and he falls forward. On his face is the expression of angry bewilderment, like a seagull just took a crap on his lunch. When he hits the pavement, I run to him and kick the knife out of his hands. People running towards us is the last thing I see before I fall forward onto concrete that rips the skin from my palms, which does not slow my forward motion enough to prevent my forehead from crashing into the curb.

    Time must be passing without me because the pain in my temple is all that exists until the elderly woman, clutching her purse anew, pulls me up from the ground on the pavement. She kisses me on the cheek and holds the back of my head which is drenched in sweat. A small circle has formed around.... well, me, I guess. A small circle has formed around me.

    And a small circle has formed around someone else. But my circle is thick with people and I can't see who is in the other circle. Instinctively, I scan my circle to see if she's somewhere here, but of course, she's not. That sort of impulse will fade. This is a world filled with women and sooner or later I'll be thinking about one of them, looking for her in the crowd when someone calls me.

"How's it feel to be a hero?" An oily man with cowboy boots and southern rasp walks up to me and shakes my hand. He is the perfect guy to deliver that line to me, I will just be grateful that he's a part of this. The old woman still has me by the shoulder and she's taken a tissue out of her bag to apply to my forehead. I'm disappointed that there is so little blood, but still grateful there is some blood. Without a good cut for a face bandage, way less people are going to ask, "What happened?"

Standing on the tops of my toes, I make out The Boy With the Knife who is now The Boy in Handcuffs. He's not being led away, but just kinda posing with two police officers for some reporters that have gathered around him.

I'm pulled down from the tops of my toes by a young woman with a pad and paper. She gets my attention by waving carefully painted nails in front of my face. Because I never understand the first thing a pretty woman says, I ask her to repeat herself.

"So, you see this teenager take from the woman and you go after the teenager?" she asks.

"Sí," I tell her, even though she's speaking to me in English.

"And then you fall and you hurt?"

"Sí," I say, realizing she's a reporter, "Muy mal."

A bearded Guatemalan kneels a few feet in front of me and takes my picture. A pack of giggling teenage girls points phones at me. The shoeshine boys from the park are sitting on their boxes, giggling at me. The lovely reporter grabs my hand, "So, you not afraid of the knife."

"No," I say to her, "I was muy, muy afraid."

Soon the photographers, who had been taking photos of the Boy in Handcuffs, are swarming around me, clicking their cameras weapon-like.

"You write your name, age, and your nationality here," the reporter says batting her eyelashes and handing me her notebook.

"You bet I will," I say taking the pad. I think I see Stella's face in-between two onlookers, but after I blink, she's gone and was never there. It's just my mind searching for what it won't find. A police officer pushes his way between the reporters and asks me a few questions through the reporter who translates. They want to know what they already know.

The boy mugged the woman and then I ran after him and knocked him down and he dropped his knife.

The reporter tells me that her name is Liliana and then with a big smile informs me that the police have found drugs on the boy and because he had a weapon he is going to have problems. I ask how old he is, but they don't know the answer to that.

"Great," I say, noticing every detail of the scars on his face.

Liliana asks, "So why did you do what you did?"

And to answer that question I'd have to tell the story of my whole life. I'd need to say how exhausting it is being a coward. I'd have to explain how I was bursting to do anything other than what I'd been doing. I'd need to say how I knew inside that this kid was the boy whose life I saved from a worse fate at the hands of Quay and Co. But there's no way to relate any of this, so instead, I say, "I just reacted. I didn't think about it."

CHAPTER TWENTY-FIVE

I'm not going to leave without saying it. I just want her to understand how unfair all of this is. I don't care if she wants to know my story or not. I need to tell her because it would be easier to just leave and not say anything. She needs to know that you can bruise people without knowing it. I need her to know. I have so little time left. Nineteen hours before a shuttle takes me to the airport. I can't leave ghosts in another place. I don't want to walk off a plane filled with new regrets.

There is liberation in leaving. I have not yet arrived anywhere and the future is still unrefined. On the way to Stella's apartment, I pass through the park. It took a very reluctant Sara to get the information out of her.

"Why do you want to know?" She asked me dubiously.

"Please," I told her, sounding more desperate than I wanted. "I'm leaving tomorrow. Please, Sara."

She had sighed and my stomach twisted because I could tell she would relent. I want to turn back and forget this. But I see the pigeons scampering and the same impulse that caused me to say nothing to Quay, beckons me onwards.

But there is no need to walk beyond the park. She is already here. With her head down she is sitting on the park bench, with a book, instead of a bag of birdseed, in her hand—Emerson's *Self Reliance* the cover reveals.

She's seen me but acts like she hasn't, hiding behind the book shoved in front of her face. For the third time, I see her eyes flash over the top of her book. I've already rehearsed my exit line, "Look me up if your travels ever take you to the Northwest of the US." Then I'll stand up, without hugging her, and just walk away.

"How's the book?" I ask putting my finger on the top of its spine.

"What?" She looks around at where the noise could be coming from. "Oh, it's you."

"It's what's left of me. I'm outta here. A shuttle's coming tomorrow morning to take me away... guess I'll be quitting town before you, huh?"

I sit down next to her and she doesn't turn away from her book.

"No birdseed?"

She pats her purse, "I'm not sure they are going to get any today. They should learn that you don't always get what you want."

"That will be a very hungry lesson for them," I move an inch closer.

"Do you know what I like about people with shrunken head collections?" She closes her book and lets it sink into the folds of her dark green dress.

"What?"

"They're breaking the law."

I stop my tongue from throwing back the lighthearted response my mind automatically conjures up. This is goodbye. I stand up. "Well, I got a lot of stuff to close up before I jet out tomorrow. Look me up if your travels ever take you to the Northwest of the US."

She pulls a small bag of birdseed from her purse and throws a handful to the impatient pigeons at her feet. A tremble in her lower lip spreads to mine. I've said my exit line. I sit back down anyways.

She looks at my chest, "Do people still 'look people up' these days?"

"Well Google me, or find me on Facebook, walk through the streets shouting my name. Whatever."

"I don't think my travels will ever take me back to The States. And I'll never join Facebook."

"Well, mine might take me back around here. I want to learn Spanish so that I know what the hell everyone's been saying to time. I worry that people are making fun of me in Spanish."

"Oh they totally are," she shows me a hint of a smile.

Pretty girls like this make us crazy. Her hair isn't reckless today. It's carefully combed the way it would be if she were going to a funeral and this makes her sad blue eyes stand out even more. That must have been why I noticed her over everyone else in the bar that night. She'd be easy to fall for. It doesn't make us right for each other, it just means that I saw something in her eyes that I felt inside myself—like something I had lost.

"I've given most of them names," she says next.

"Most of who?"

"Most of the pigeons. They have names. That really greedy one over there is Spartacus. The one with some of his feathers ripped out is Helen. The white one is Hope. That one who walks with a limp is Oprah."

"You named one of your pigeons Oprah?"

"Well, there's a lot of pigeons and I started to run out of names. Geraldine over there is weird. Some days she looks overweight and other days she seems to be starving."

She throws another handful. Hope is the only one I can easily recognize as she maneuvers between the darker feathered forms, anxious for food.

"See that one over there who just sorta watches the other pigeons and doesn't care about the birdseed? That's Stella."

"I can't really see the likeness."

"She's like the bird version of me."

"Well," I say, "I don't have a lot of time."

"I named her Stella on my first day here. That's when I decided to start calling myself Stella."

Hope walks over to me, closer than the others dare, inches from my tennis shoes. She continues throwing birdseed and when I stand up her voice sinks to a remorseful hum. "Whenever I arrive somewhere new, I give myself a new name," she takes a deep breath and what I feel in my stomach is what I imagine she feels, because I know what it's like to talk about the things you don't talk about.

I stay silently standing, allowing space for her to continue. "My real name is Gertrude. Which I hate. It's a grandma's name. Ironic since my grandmas were named Jessica and Katie…not grandma names at all. In high school they called me G-turd. Which is a shitty nickname when you are insecure and have no breasts. But then my breasts came in…" She throws a healthy grab of birdseed and the pigeons fan out.

"My name was Candy for two years," her eyes stay on the pigeons, "Two very long years, Liam. My parents were Mormon. Well, I guess they still are Mormon, as far as I know. I'm sure they're still Mormons. I know they will never change that; they'd prefer to stay with the church than standby their daughter. I'm from Salt Lake City."

She pats the bench next to her and I sit down again. I am turned away from her at the same angle she is turned away from me. She is speaking in a monotone, computer voice. She hasn't even said anything so horrible yet, but my heartbeat begins to sprint—she is telling the story of what broke her.

"They were so strict, Liam. Everything was one way. That was it. I stopped believing in all of it pretty early on. Like ten. But of course I never let them know. You are not allowed to not believe. So I went through the motions. No big deal. I was not allowed to have boyfriends, so I didn't tell my parents about the ones I had. I planned to go off to college somewhere far away from my parent's control. Eighteen and I'd be free. My parents didn't see it like that. The laws of the state come second to the laws of God, they said. They wanted me to marry the son of a friend of the family. A very successful young man, they said.

"I think, like hell, I am going to marry him. It's not like, the Middle Ages. Like, people can't force anyone to marry someone. But they can strongly recommend that you do things, and my parents never saw anything they wanted me to do as optional. So I got on a bus and went to Nevada and never saw them again."

The birds have returned but she has forgotten them. "It wasn't hard to get a job as a waitress. It was not hard to get a dumpy apartment and an exciting life and new friends who could drink caffeinated pop and beer and do drugs and have sex and just be people the way people are supposed to be and not the way my parents told me to be and. . ."

She stops until I prod her to go on, "And?"

"Someone came in one day. He wanted things on the menu that we didn't have. He told me I was beautiful and could be a model and he was dressed very nicely and he was young and I didn't have anyone and he gave me a $100 tip and his card and he told me to call him and I did.

"Later that night I looked at myself in the mirror and I didn't really see what he saw. I looked myself right in the eyes and wondered if I could really be that—beautiful. Just because you always thought that you were ugly doesn't mean that you haven't become beautiful while no one was watching. So he took me out to dinner, told me that 'it'd be a tragedy to waste a face like that.' And Liam, I didn't want a tragedy on my hands.

"It was then that I remembered those forgotten dreams of becoming an actress. This is how stuff like that happens, I told myself. You work hard and wonder when you'll get a break and finally a man walks in leaves you a $100 tip and tells you he can help you. So you believe him. First a model, and then an actress, he says. How surprised would my parents be to see me suddenly on TV?

So he arranged for me to go to Vegas. Las Vegas! And I become a model all right. And the people there are very convincing, but not very nice. And they paid for my apartment there. So you justify it to yourself, that there's nothing wrong with being an underwear model. Lots of actresses got their start this way, you tell yourself, but you don't know if that's true.

"The studio was not what you expected. Nothing was. Mike, the guy in the suit who arranged it all, disappears. His phone becomes disconnected. I never see him again. And the studio is more like a dingy apartment. So you're an underwear model for a little while. And you tell yourself that you are just doing this for now. And they pay you, but not as much as Mike said they would, and the city is expensive. And so you're this underwear model. But this is just how they get you to become a topless model.

And after you are a topless model, you start to realize that you are not a model at all. And pretty soon you are a lot of things you thought you were not at all. You start taking their drugs. The ones you swore you would never take when they first offered. And you tell yourself that you are not in the porn business, but of course, you are. Sometimes there's not even a camera rolling and you're just a whore.

"At that point you just stop fighting whatever they want you to do because they are going to get you to do it sooner or later. They are so, so, very persuasive. After that none of your choices feel like choices, it's all just part of this horrible ride you don't know how you got on or how to get off."

Her hands are trembling too much to grab hold of much birdseed. I reach for her hand but she pushes mine away and continues: "You work with other 'models' who are working with you, and you are working with them, and yes you signed some contracts but who knows what the hell they said and pretty soon you are all over the Internet and they pay you a little better and usually you just stay home in your apartment and take the pills because you are ashamed to go out because sometimes when you do, people recognize you, and you had no idea how many people have seen you, so you want to hide from everyone. And different parts of you compete to make you feel either pride or shame at being recognized. Shame always wins. And so when people come up to you in a bar and say that you look familiar, you do—they've seen you on the Internet—and you leave before they can figure that out."

She stops. Turned away from me, she looks back and forth between the ground and the horizon.

"Liam," she says, emptying the bag until every last seed has fallen, "I wish I could go back and remake those choices, being the person I am now. But that's what everyone always wishes. To have do-overs. And do you know how much time you can spend rethinking one shitty decision?"

"It doesn't matter," I tell her, needing something else to say.

"Our whole damn lives. The whole goddamn rest of our lives, Liam. You can spend the whole goddamn rest of your life thinking about one do-over. But you can't do it over. So God damn it!"

I need her to understand something I've been desperately trying to convince myself of. "It's all over, all that's over. And I bet your parents still love you and want to know where you are."

She jerks her head and stares at me with horrible eyes. "I didn't get out because I left. I wasn't strong enough. I got out because I got something that made me a hazard. In my work they call something the show stopper," she pauses and I see my mom in her drowning eyes. "If you don't have the courage to get yourself out, you can bet that when one of the regular lab reports that they have you do comes back saying that you have the show stopper, the show stops. The goddamn show stops, Liam. The lights come on, and you really, really realize your own recklessness and you really, really see what it is that you have been doing. And that's exactly how it happened. The labs came back and the show stopped."

She gives the empty birdseed bag to the wind and the pigeons step back. "The show stopper is HIV. You get it? Funny, huh? Because it like, stops the whole show."

Her locked doors, the ones I tried to pry into, swing open and an absurd nudity glares from somewhere deep inside her and I see her for the first time.

To have one goddamn do-over.

She's too strong for her eyes, which want to cry, "So you see, I'm not dating material, you follow? Get it? And it's better that my parents never know what happened to their daughter than to know who she is. I can't believe I just told you all of this. I'm dead eventually, like everyone else, so I prefer to be dead to them now so I can at least live my life in a simple way and make it as beautiful as anyone else can. They have other kids. I miss my brothers and sisters, but I'm not their sister anymore. I'm not the person who ran away from home six years ago. She caused me, but she's not me and I'm not her. So here I am and here we are."

"Stella." I say, wondering if I should call her Gertrude now, "I'm sorry."

"Me too."

"You and me. I don't care. You have AIDS and—"

"I have HIV, not AIDS. Jesus."

"Okay," I keep my voice slow and firm, "you have that then. And here you are and here I am, and that's just where things in the world are right now." I look at the sheltered sky and try to say something more. But what is there except more pointless words? Words, words, words. Stupid little words. "I'm sorry if I'm trying to say something. I guess we naturally always want to be able to fix everything."

She wipes away what could have been tears. "Do me a favor and don't spend too much of your emotional capital on all this. Do yourself a favor and just leave me with my pigeons and go home and be happy. My life is the way it is because this is the way I want it to be. Situations like this kill me, okay? So now you know why I am how I am and just don't say anything to me. I am not unhappy. I am the happiest I have ever been. I still have years to be happy. I'm on the right medications, this thing isn't the death curse it used to be. So now I want to walk down my road happy and alone. Go home, Liam. Go see your mom. Tell her you love her and hug her."

She takes out a notebook from her purse and writes on a scrap of paper, "Friendship is all I have to give and I don't give it to many people. Email me. Be my friend, etcetera."

She stands up and I do too. I look into her stormy eyes underneath the dark clouds looming over Antigua. We hug. At first it seems like the embrace is going to be quick and awkward. But as we pull away we reach again for each other to hold. Our hug seems less about holding, and more about making a declaration that even the hardest hardships are not immortal. Storms come, but eventually, they go. They leave damage when they tear through us, but they also leave things still standing, and lives cannot help but rebuild with what pieces are left. They can't take this away and I whisper three words I've never said to anyone. It is hard. Our embrace. Love. Life. Everything. But it is beautiful. Stella. Or, Gertrude. Our embrace. The smell of her hair, the smallness of her hands, and the touch of her tears against my fingertips as I wipe them off her cheeks as quickly as they come. I love her and know now that love's expression is not something specific, but anything real, anything true. Tears burn from her eyes. Their heat burns months of my own difficulty away.

And for the first time in six months, on a cinematic cue, the dry season ends and rain begins to pelt the city with a cathartic ferocity. We embrace beneath the torrential furry as the pigeons and people scurry away to find shelter. And beneath the falling water, Stella starts shaking. At first I think she is sobbing, but she is laughing. She laughs and says something about the rain. I hug her harder, hoping that time will be kind enough to stop forever, since it is moments like this that we live for anyway. It is moments like this that we are lucky to have a half dozen of in our long lifetimes.

With my arm around her, we walk into the café off from the park in soaking clothes. "They better have a lot of coffee," she whispers to my shoulder that she has turned into her pillow. Everything has changed. Now we know each other's stories, and share modest parts of each other's lives. And maybe that's why everything feels so much lighter, because Stella is carrying heavy parts of my story just as I have lifted her heavy secrets into accepting arms. Through each other, we have both been lifted to a place neither of us could have climbed on our own.

CHAPTER TWENTY-SIX

When I go to confirm my shuttle, I see a sign at the travel agency offering tours of *Ciudad Vieja*. This is where Stella insisted I visit the *basurero*, which I've since learned is the word for a garbage dump. I wonder if I even have time. The sign says that it is only twenty minutes away. I have already checked out of my hostel. My suitcase is safely behind the travel agency's counter.

In choppy English, the man behind the counter tells me there is time, but that they do not have any tours scheduled for today. For fifty dollars, he says, I can rent a private shuttle that will take me there and then directly to the airport. I pay and we are off, flying through bustling streets one last time while my mind sprints to keep up with everything racing in and out of it.

The driver looks confused when I ask him to drive me to the city's garbage dump. Like he must not understand something in the English. But a twenty-dollar bill makes him shrug and drive down a dirt road that leads to it. He pulls off to the side of the road and points, telling me in broken English that he will wait for me in the shuttle. I wonder if he is going to just drive off and steal my baggage, and decide I don't care if he does.

Something is very wrong here. The muddy trail is obscured by a smoke-choked horizon that shrouds everything in front of me. I cough and move towards what I thought were hills, but turn out to be mounds of garbage. I try to remember Dante's *Inferno*, because that seems an apt reference point. In the garbage dump, at the foot of the volcano *Fuego*, is the world's final stop. There is no place further, or lower, to go. The distant eruptions of the volcano that make for scenic panoramas from the vantage point of Antigua are brutal outbursts here. And the smells. Smells strongly chemical, sulfuric, mixed with rotting organic scents, the corpses of decaying dogs tossed about and burning plastic overwhelm my nose and sting my eyes.

Rejected things burn in mountains of flaming garbage. It's not the refuse, not the smoke, not the putrid smells, not the dog carcasses, or the rats, or flies, that makes me break into a million guilty pieces. It's young girls and little boys I see picking through the garbage, wading through the smoke. The refuse of the world is boys. The refuse of the world is girls. They appear from and disappear into smoky swarms of flies, laying claim to the squalor.

No one seems to notice a lone gringo in their midst. They go about their task of picking through the garbage mechanically. Something is wrong with everyone. In the city beggars begged with outstretched hands, eagerness, energy, with pleading eyes, there was something close to hope in their eyes. And even that was just barely tolerable. But that's not here. Here no one approaches me and this is so much worse. The eyes are empty and turn away. They can see that I don't belong here and am just an apparition from some other world.

How can little girls in the 21st century be barefoot in a garbage dump sifting through trash? Where are their parents? What are their names? Why hasn't someone taken care of these things? And how will we fix it?

Here are the sons and daughters of Mayan kings and queens. If our world leaders are busy solving the problems of the world, why isn't this solved? Why was I allowed to spend half a year of my life feeling such sorrow for myself at the same time shit like this was going on?

You've seen the ads asking for a monthly donation.
But commercials can't take you to places like this.
They take you as far as you will allow them to.
They don't take you here.
But you did.

I can't keep him away any longer. I can't help it. I think of my dad. Of my mom, and wonder if she really believes he's in hell. Without straining, without overwhelming grief, I manage to hold a picture of him in my head, and there he is, smiling in that image, somewhere inside of me.

Maybe he didn't want to die. Maybe he just had five bad minutes. That's all it takes, five bad minutes. He loved that car; the idea of taking something wrecked and making it live again. When it appeared in our garage in our perfect little blue house, we didn't know. We couldn't see what he was crafting as he sanded off the rust to find the car underneath.

In just a moment, less than five minutes, decisions that a lifetime should not be sufficient to decide can be made. If he had really wanted to die, the TiVO would not have been programmed to record The Duck's game. If he had wanted to die, he would not have left me to find the body he no longer needed. Five minutes is so short, but long enough to destroy anything in this easy-to-shatter life.

It was no one's fault, the therapist told me, you can't blame yourself. Well, it was his fault, there's no denying that, I corrected her, remembering every phone call I didn't return, every cruel word I ever spoke to him, sure that if I had called him or visited more often it never would have come to this.

Instead of focusing on the fact that your father died, see past all that and remember that he lived, she said. In just a few minutes decisions can be made. Beethoven never had more than one moment to do things with two hands and two broken ears. Hitler had a broken mind and never more than a moment.

Remember that he lived, she said. And I did remember and I do remember. Today I do. He lived for me and for Chris and for mom. He lived for that car, and he loved to care for it and us and he was not just making something real out of something dead but maybe he was trying to fix something that had broken inside him after Chris didn't come home.

It was no one's fault, she said. But she was only repeating things textbooks told her to say, she being so young for a psychiatrist. No, I said to her, I think it was probably his fault. After all, he was the one who closed the garage door, and he was the one who started that car and just sat there until he conceded the point of living to exhaust fumes. And he had been waiting for fifteen years to start that car.

He closed the garage door in our little blue house's garage, he started the engine. And all it took was five minutes. In five really bad minutes you can do really bad things to others and to yourself and he was depressed and at least he only did a bad thing to himself, but I guess he also did a really bad thing to others because here I am and there is no one left in my family to talk to my mom.

I think about Chris. I hate the term "friendly-fire" they used to describe the official cause of death. We were brothers, but we were also strangers, with our own lives and viewpoints. He had the army, and I was going to college and I had my life and he had his life and we were little pieces of each other's.

"Never stop being inspired," was the last thing I remember my dad saying to me. We were talking on the phone. It seemed at the time good fatherly advice for a son who had just finished college and was about to embark on what everyone calls life.

In death they share the same spirit. I don't know how to grieve for them separately; their individual tragedies melt into one vast sea. And out there, under its sad swells, I can always dive deeper and deeper. But no matter how deep I seem to dive, I always come back up for air. I'm forced to see both their faces pass through my mind. I have less to go home to than the little I left behind.

Dad only believed in that stupid war because he believed in Chris, so after he was killed there was very little inspiration to go around in our little blue house. Mom had her religion, but dad always just went through the motions of that. All he had was a dead son, so after he retired and finished the car, there must not have been anything left to do.

Maybe he could have gotten past those hopeless minutes. But he didn't, because sometimes, I guess, it's just too much.

"Remember that he lived," my therapist said, "and not how he died." And I try every day and today I am succeeding in remembering who he was and not just how he died. It is only after someone has been gone for a while, when instead of seeing what's lost, you start to see what parts are still left. There are still pictures of my unbroken family hanging in the living room of the house I grew up in. There are pictures in my mending mind, hanging down alleyways of thoughts that I am still relearning to walk through. Those pictures, these images used to represent something real. What part of that is him? What is a shooting star years after it has fallen? Why is it that the same atmosphere that loves and protects us kisses death to the rocks of Space?

And my mom is still so alive, but she seems like just a body. Where is the happy woman who raised me? Inside of me a million previous versions of self have slipped away to make room for me—for better or worse. Maybe in the days to come, when I have stepped aside to make room for new selves, they will have it in them to be inspired.

My brother was in the wrong place at the wrong time, and my dad was maybe just the meager victim of that too—the victim of five utterly uninspiring, but I guess forgivable, minutes.

In the thick, rubbery smoke, the garbage pickers continue to materialize then disappear back into the chemical darkness. How can the same world of beauty and abundance also be the world of this place and these people? Lost lives, but still, they walk. Dead, dying lives, but still, they search, looking for something to eat.

Along with every other incomprehensible thing here, there is music and it does not make sense here any more than the people do. What is this music? The music, completely unsuitable, entirely out of place, is hidden inside the smoke. Someone nearby is playing the guitar and singing words I don't understand. Blossoming beneath the violent booms of the volcano is a gentle melody that is soothing and fighting back against all the viciousness of this place, the world.

I walk through the smoke towards the melody. Soft notes of the acoustic guitar compete with the hum of swarming flies and the tenor voice of an angel. It is singing something so lovely that the tears never had a chance of staying behind my eyes. I venture an absurd thought: angel, it's an angel.

Through the walls of garbage, I walk. Above me the volcano is impossibly large and majestically violent. Towards music, I walk. And places like this must have existed since civilization's dawn.One man's garbage is always another's only means of survival.

I think of ancient Greece and wonder if it was any different from modern-day anywhere. Maybe everything that is happening has always happened, and will continue to happen again and again and again. A semi-circle of a dozen ragged people appears from the smoke. Half are seated, the rest standing, all so ragged. Mostly children and a few adults, all obscured by the smoke. One woman holds a baby underneath her coat and closes her eyes, facing the source of the music. Someone is seated in the center. The music is too beautiful to be possible here or anywhere. And this music is doing something. It is reaching as far as it attempts to reach, painting for me fully that fleeting image of life that has always darted just out of my reach. The people have come to listen to Pablo.

It's his gift to them. It's how one guitar can save the world. He is the someone seated at the center on a five-gallon bucket with a shabby guitar in his hands. I stop a few feet away and immerse myself in the moment. Pablo's head is bowed and his eyes closed. Soft lyrics in that beautiful language I do not understand enough of are soaring from his lips.

If places like this have always existed, then so too has Pablo. As I stand staring, Pablo's eyes fall upon me like a blessing, and his smile is an ocean my tears flow to. He holds me in his illuminating grin, nods, and turns from me to carry on his song to the joyful vagrants around him. He has it. He carries the cure to all this smoke and poverty. It's within us. Out of the smoke, his music rings. I look deep inside and see further than I ever have. I see beyond the darkness that's blinded me from so much for so long. It is time to go. Time to listen to Stella and hug my mother. Time to clear the slate and fill it with the right sort of things. Time to smile, because smiling is better than not smiling. I will not leave this music here. I will take it and make Pablo's music my music. And my music too will cut through the smoke. And if I can make tomorrow a little better than yesterday, then I think I have a shot. I think we all do.

I turn to walk to the shuttle. I am not ready to leave Guatemala and wonder if I'll be on that flight. I won't need a guitar, because I can think of a thousand other ways of making that beautiful music. This is something. This is something very new. And it's not a great end to anything, but I think it could be an okay beginning—a something to somewhere.

The End

Books & Music by Luke Maguire Armstrong

Thanks for your kind support!

POETRY

iPoems for the Dolphins to Click Home About (2010)

How We Are Human (2012)

Bushwick Poetry (2013)

All the Beloved Known Things (2019)

The Starlight Still Within Us (2021)

NON-FICTION

Amazing Grace For Survivors (2008)

The Nomad's Nomad (2015)

FICTION

How One Guitar Will Save the World (2021)

BLOG
www.TravelWriteSing.com

MUSIC
@ALEKOSHATITLAN

Albums

Skipping Stones (2021) Milarepa! (2021)

EPs

Celestial Reasoning (2021) Mantras (2021)

 Thanks for your kind support!

POETRY

 iPoems for the Dolphins to Click Home About (2010)

How We Are Human (2012)

Bushwick Poetry (2013)

 All the Beloved Known Things (2019)

 The Starlight Still Within Us (2021)

NON-FICTION

Amazing Grace For Survivors (2008)

The Nomad's Nomad (2015)

FICTION

How One Guitar Will Save the World (2021)

BLOG
www.TravelWriteSing.com

MUSIC
@ALEKOSHATITLAN

Albums
Skipping Stones (2021)   Milarepa! (2021)

EPs
Celestial Reasoning (2021)   Mantras (2021)

Printed in Great Britain
by Amazon